BEDLAM IN THE KITCHEN

Out in the dining room a phone had fallen to the floor. Teddy crawled over and found the receiver, punching the numbers 911. Immediately an operator answered.

"There's a dead woman here." Teddy's breath came in spasms. "I'm at a house on Potter Road out past Deming."

"What is your house number, please?"

"I don't know. It's three miles outside of town and there's an iron wheel holding up the mailbox from an old wagon."

"Don't hang up."

Teddy glanced again at the body. Now there were two long smears of blood across the vinyl following her into the dining room. The knees of her gabardine slacks were capped in brown ooze.

"What's your name, please?" asked the dispatcher.

"Teodora Morelli. How long 'til you get here?"

"Does the victim require first aid?"

"She's dead! Somebody cut her arteries."

TALKING RAIN

A PROFESSOR TEODORA MORELLI MYSTERY

LINDA FRENCH

AVON BOOKS NEW YORK

AVON BOOKS
A division of
The Hearst Corporation
1350 Avenue of the Americas
New York, New York 10019

Copyright © 1998 by Linda French
Published by arrangement with the author
Visit our website at **http://www.AvonBooks.com**
Library of Congress Catalog Card Number: 97-94320
ISBN: 0-380-79573-6

First Avon Books Printing: April 1998

AVON TRADEMARK REG. U.S. PAT. OFF. AND IN OTHER COUNTRIES, MARCA REGISTRADA, HECHO EN U.S.A.

Printed in the U.S.A.

WCD   10 9 8 7 6 5 4 3 2 1

**To Paul
Firstborn**

1

Perfecta, Goddess of Love, let out a blood-curdling cry and caught Tabor the Amazon in a flying body scissors. Black-clad Tabor snarled like a cur and collapsed on the mat, hauling Perfecta down on top of her. Perfecta's minuscule toga flapped up from her fanny to reveal a gold lamé brief the size of a tissue. The audience, shocked at the sight of chaste Perfecta's buns, exploded in wild appreciation.

Down in the third row of Vancouver's Pacific Coliseum, Teddy Morelli sprang to her feet to give maximum authority to her five-foot-three-inch frame. "Get up, Tabor! Get up." Behind Teddy a little boy hooted through a rolled-up program, "Finishing move, Perfecta. Send her to Hades!"

Teddy turned and glared. "That's not very nice. Just because Tabor's wearing black doesn't mean she's a bad person." The astonished child climbed down from his folding chair and stood next to his teenage brother.

Springing from the mat, Tabor grabbed Perfecta's hair and dragged the celestial goddess painfully to her feet. The crowd booed and Tabor raised a black-fringed arm in defiance.

Teddy stared open-mouthed at her sister, Tabor the Amazon, formerly Miss Pacific Northwest HardBody and lately, assistant basketball coach at University of Washington. The costumers had clad Tabor's glorious six-foot frame

1

in a black tanksuit so tight it looked as if she had grown three sizes since putting it on. Her muscled calves were strapped into knee-high buskins and circling her knotty biceps were fringed leather bands imprinted with silver medallions.

Growling and twitching, Tabor strutted around the ring, her toned rump flexing like a pony's. Meanwhile, white-clad Perfecta lithely climbed the turnbuckles and stood poised on the top rope.

"Hades! Hades!" chanted the throng.

Perfecta signaled "thumbs up" to the crowd and leaped into the air, landing—astonishingly—in Tabor's open arms. Tabor crumpled under the weight. As Perfecta skittered away, Tabor staggered to her feet in a blind haze, then she spotted Perfecta. She lunged like a bull.

With sprightly grace, Perfecta leaned over and locked her arms around Tabor's middle. Aided by the Amazon's own velocity, the little goddess flipped Tabor upside down, then tossed her through the ropes to the thick mats on the floor. Tabor landed painfully, writhing in agony, her legs jerking like a galvanized frog's. The crowd roared with delight. Hades, at last.

Wrapping up for the finale, Perfecta flitted jubilantly around the ring as the groggy Amazon crawled back onto the mat. Perfecta, with a twist of her wrist, rolled Tabor on her back while the ref quickly counted three. The crowd erupted in a roar and the referee held up Perfecta's lithe little arm in triumph. Lethargically, the defeated Amazon picked up her black cape and broadsword and stumbled up the center aisle. Teddy left to follow.

As Tabor disappeared through the backstage curtain, a pot-bellied security guard positioned himself squarely in front of Teddy, his arms across his chest.

"I'm with Tabor the Amazon," she said.

The guard's eyes said he was used to uppity little brunettes who lied in his face. "Get out of the way. Here comes the next match." He swept Teddy off to the side as the spotlight splashed light on the curtains. Sinister music filled the air and out strode two bearded behemoths in bearskins sneering and hissing at the crowd. Teddy watched stupefied as the wrestlers tormented patrons on the center aisle. The guard touched her elbow. "What's your name?"

"Teddy Morelli."

"Wait here." The guard disappeared, leaving Teddy to stare at the lighted ring where "The Juneau Boys" were taunting the crowd with bear claws.

Suddenly the security guard appeared. "The women are at the end of the hall." He swept her through the curtain.

Down the dingy corridor Teddy passed open dressing room doors. Inside, burly wrestlers in various states of undress chatted with their wives and managers. In one room, a child of six sat coloring at a dressing table, totally uninterested in the near-naked men in the mirror.

At the end of the hall, Teddy knocked and listened.

Perfecta opened the door. Already clad in a black tee shirt and leopard-print leggings, the goddess had accessorized her outfit with cork wedgies and a live ferret. The gleaming animal had at least two feet of backbone, and either Perfecta or the ferret smelled like the elephant cage at the zoo. The animal routed under Perfecta's bleached hair as the goddess sized up Teddy. "Honey, you can't be back here. I sign autographs on the way out." The accent was pure Texas.

"Short Girl!" Tabor called from the depths of the dressing room. "Come on in."

Teddy straightened her shoulders and, with as much dignity as she could muster, strode across the room.

Tabor was slumped wearily in a folding chair and used her foot to pull out a second one for Teddy. "I'd give you a hug, except I'm all sweaty." Tabor held up a toned calf. "Look what these buskins are doing to my leg."

Teddy sat down and examined her sister's calf. At regular intervals, where the five straps had cut into Tabor's flesh, were fresh blisters, some fluid-filled and ready to be lanced. Under the blisters was the angry skin of last week's wounds.

"Tabor, you've got to stop wearing those sandals."

"Can't. They're the best part of my costume."

"Get some black hightops. Très camp."

"Très get-me-fired." Tabor kicked off a sandal. "So, what did you think of the show?"

Teddy grimaced. "Are you always going to be the bad guy?"

"You mean 'the heel.' " Tabor ripped off her headband. "Perfecta's our 'baby face.' I'm the heel." She called loudly across the room. "But that doesn't mean Perfecta's always gonna win, does it, Perfecta?"

"Like hell." In the mirror Perfecta stroked her spiky eyelashes with a mascara wand. "I'll be damned if I'm gonna have you sitting on top of me." Under the harsh yellow light the goddess's pancake makeup could not conceal the road map of her forty-five years.

"We still need feedback," added Tabor. "Let us know if you're not seeing something you want."

"Umm." Teddy looked away.

Heavy pounding suddenly rattled the walls. Without warning the door flew open and a three-hundred-pound personification of Popeye the Sailorman walked in. The seaman was dressed in white bell-bottoms and a gob hat. On his feet were red hightop sneakers.

"Steamboat, dammit!" Perfecta hollered. "Can't you wait 'til somebody says 'come in'?"

Teddy stared open-mouthed at the nautical biomass that now filled the room. Although he was not much taller than Tabor's six feet, Steamboat had at least four times her girth. His hammy arms lay like hot water bottles against his flanks. His rotund belly said that he did much of his training at the dinner table. Scanning the room, he stopped, copper eyes softening as they rested on Tabor. "Hi, Cutie. How'd it go?"

Tabor sniffed, "I wasn't watching. Ask Perfecta."

In the mirror Perfecta fussed over the flawless red cupid's bow on her upper lip. "Still not showcasing her moves. She'll work it out, though."

Steamboat beamed like a proud father. "Of course she will. She's got more potential than anyone in the business— male or female."

The celestial goddess dropped her lip brush into her denim bag and hoisted it onto her shoulder. Pulling the ferret out from under her tee shirt, she plumped him close to her face. "Well, bye, y'all. See you Monday." Perfecta sashayed out the door.

In the silence Steamboat's gaze fell awkwardly on Teddy. Tabor saw she would have to do introductions, and said peevishly, "Teddy, this is Steamboat Stevens, former Canadian National Powerlifting champion. Steamboat, this is my sister. First time she's seen me wrestle."

Teddy stood and tendered her hand to the immense brute. "How do you do?"

Gently enclosing her metacarpals in his mammoth paw, Steamboat protected them from harm. "I bet you're pretty proud of Tabor, huh?" Pressing lightly, he disengaged his hand as delicately as a well-paid physician. "What'd you say your name was?"

"Teddy."

Steamboat eyed her tight little torso. "May I pick you up?"

"No!" She planted her feet, just in case.

"Sorry." He reddened. "You work out?"

"I try. I used to be a gymnast."

"Hey, outstanding! 'The Morelli Sisters.' Wouldn't that look great on the bill? The mucky-mucks are always looking for high production values."

"Steamboat," Tabor snickered. "Teddy's a history professor."

"Oh," he murmured. "I'm *so* sorry." Dropping to a chair, Steamboat tilted back, watching Tabor ransack her locker. "Hey, Cutie, I heard you wiped out all the women's lifting records at Rollo's yesterday."

Tabor snapped over her shoulder, "They were set by wusses."

Eyes half-closed with pleasure, Steamboat watched Tabor rummage through her clothes. "You know, I could tell Tabor was a professional the first time she walked into Rollo's. She went over to the leg press and decked up three hundred fifty kilograms. Positioned her feet to work through all the quads."

Tabor banged the locker door. "I was showing off." She strode to a chair in the corner and turned her back on them, pulling down the straps of her tanksuit.

Teddy and Steamboat watched the exquisite rise and fall of Tabor's latissimus dorsi as she pulled an extra-long sweatshirt over her head. Under it disappeared her wasp waist. In a dreamy voice, Steamboat asked, "Cutie, want me to show you my Boston crab?" He caught his reflection in the mirror and tipped his gob hat rakishly forward.

"Only if you can do it without pawing the hell out of me."

"I don't paw," he pouted.

Not bothering with underwear, Tabor wiggled into jeans and did a short belly dance to zip them up. Pacing to the door, she said, "Be right back, Teddy. Then we can go." She swept out of the room and a radiant Steamboat turned to Teddy. "Isn't she something?"

"Something," Teddy agreed.

"You know, you and Tabor really ought to work up a tag team, Mutt-and-Jeff kinda thing. I bet you could really set some sensational moves."

"Oh, yes." She smiled broadly. "I can just see the chair-

man of my department when I tell him I'm trying to break
into professional wrestling.''

"Naw, no kidding. It's a *great* career. Can't beat the
people. They'd give you the shirts off their backs. And if
you make it big—boy,'' he shook his head, "people at the
top make millions. Of course, the big money's in merchan-
dising, got to market yourself. You know how much Hulk
Hogan makes off his kid vitamins?''

"How much?''

Steamboat sat up straight, rising to the challenge. "Oh,
I bet he makes a hundred thousand a year on that.''

"That much?''

"Yep.'' Looking at the door, he said quietly, "Can I ask
you a question?''

"Sure.''

Without warning the wrestler lumbered across the room
and peered down the hall. Coming back, he whispered,
"Do you think Tabor likes me?''

Teddy stared at Steamboat's apple cheeks hanging like
jelly bags. His strawberry-blond eyelashes blinked around
his tawny eyes. "You *do* know sh—'' Teddy changed her
mind. "Steamboat, I couldn't tell you. She's moved, and
just got a phone last week. This is the first time I've talked
to her in a couple of months.''

He checked his broad reflection in the mirror, then
sucked in his gut and struck a casual pose. "Then maybe
I will.''

"You will what?'' Tabor limped back into the room with
a barbell, two ten-pound doughnuts on each end. She
banged into the doorjamb and left a gouge in the soft wood.

"Tabor, what's the barbell for?''

"Rollo had a garage sale and I got this whole thing for
five dollars Canadian. Chrome bar, four dime plates.'' She
dipped the bar and two doughnuts clattered to the floor.

"Well, at *least* put the collars on, Tabe.'' Teddy picked
up the weights.

"It doesn't have collars. That's why it was five dollars."

"Great. So we have to carry it to my car like this?"

Tabor scooped up the bar. "I'll carry it. You take my bag."

"You can't carry the whole thing. I'll keep these." Cradling the two rings, Teddy slung Tabor's gym bag over her shoulder. "Want me to drive over and pick you up? The car's three blocks away."

"Nah, we'll be fine." Tabor slipped one of the remaining rings on the other side of the bar and jerked the whole thing onto her shoulders. "Okay, Short Girl, ready?"

"Anytime you are."

"Bye, cutie." Steamboat beamed.

"Whatever."

Teddy exchanged glances with the gentle giant. "Nice to meet you, Steamboat. Hope we meet again sometime."

"Me too."

In the hall out of earshot, Teddy murmured, "Gee, Tabor, what'd you put in his water?"

"Ridiculous, isn't he?"

"That's unfair. You really should tell him."

"I did already: gay, lesbian, queer. All he did was ask me out for blinis." Forcefully Tabor pushed her back against the exit bar on the door.

Outside winter rain fell. November chill grazed their cheeks and gooseflesh rippled down their arms. Struggling under the streetlights to Teddy's little Subaru wagon, they dumped the barbell in back and started south on the fifty-mile trip across the border to Bellingham, Washington. Warmed by the purring heater, they drove down Highway 99, windshield wipers clearing arcs of vision through the rain.

At the American customs station cars idled twenty deep, so they rolled to a stop in line. Tabor stretched luxuriously and gazed at the white Georgian Peace Arch on the lawn at the Canadian-American line. "Steamboat says he uses the border crossing at Lynden. Saves an hour when these lines are backed up.''

''Steamboat's probably right. This place has been backed up since 1974.''

For a few minutes they worked their way silently toward the customs booth, then Tabor said brightly, ''You never did say what you thought of our match. Honest, now.''

Teddy narrowed her eyes. ''You really want to know?''

''Aw, come on, Teddy. At this level it's pure entertainment.''

''Yes. I would say just about the mentality of Saturday morning TV.''

''Exactly!'' Tabor nodded vigorously. ''That's it.''

''So you don't care that you've got yourself decked out like some second-rate cartoon character?''

''Are you kidding? I'm working my *buns* off to look like a second-rate cartoon character. We're Saturday morning come to life. Get it?''

''Tabor, wrestling is suspended disbelief for morons.''

''God, you're a snob.''

''And what are *they* going to say?'' She meant their five siblings and widowed Italian mother. ''Marmee's going to vent when she hears you quit grad school.''

''I know.'' Tabor cracked her knuckles. ''That's why I wanted you to come tonight. So you could tell her it's okay.''

''Tabor, it's not okay! And I'm not going to do your dirty work for you with Marmee. We've already been through that.''

''Being a dyke is dirty?''

''Tabor, stop it.'' Pulling up to the customs booth, Teddy rolled down her window.

''Good evening, ladies.'' The cheery guard made professional eye contact. ''What's your citizenship?''

''American.''

''And what was the purpose of your visit to Canada?''

They explained the evening's activities as best they could, and when they got to the part about "goods purchased in Canada," the guard waved them away so he wouldn't have to deal with a broken barbell.

Driving the thirty miles south to Bellingham, they turned inland on the Mount Baker Highway, toward the mountains. Through the silver drizzle their headlamps bathed the shadowy woods. They drove deep into Whatcom County, where Douglas firs vaulted the road and the black hillsides rose in waves. The rain softened to sweet mizzle and Teddy switched the wipers to intermittent. Breaking the silence, she said, "So who's this woman you're living with?"

Tabor warmed visibly. "Her name's Margaret. You'll really like her. She's Canadian."

"How old is she?"

Tabor started in on her knuckles. "Fifty-five. But she's like totally clued in. She writes children's books."

"What's she doing down here?"

"She has dual citizenship from her ex-husband. She *was* trying to get some money together, but she lost her job in Bellingham about six months ago."

"And she can't find another one?"

"I don't think she really tried." Tabor started on her wrist joints. "That's how we met. She put up an ad at the Women's Alliance for a housemate to help with the rent and she just started writing again."

"Her books any good?"

"Don't know, she doesn't have any copies. I keep meaning to get to the library."

"What's her name again?" Teddy turned the wipers back up.

"Margaret Zimmerman."

"Never heard of her."

"I think she might be a little famous up in Canada. At least she knows some famous people."

"Like who?"

"Like, when CBC radio was playing Glenn Gould's 'Goldberg Variations,' she said she wondered how the family was, she hadn't seen them since the funeral."

"Wow."

"Yeah. And once, when she was knitting a pair of slippers, she said Margaret Atwood taught her how to make them when they were both teaching at U.B.C. She wasn't showing off or anything."

"Gee."

"Yeah, I consider her my mentor now. You should see some of the stuff she's having me read."

"Like what?"

"Like Barbara Ward: *Spaceship Earth, Five Ideas That Changed the World.* Also, *See Here, Mr. Feynman,* about Richard Feynman the physicist."

"Interesting." Teddy crossed the Nooksack River bridge. "Tabor, where do I turn?"

"Keep going. I'll show you when we get there."

They rolled into the logging town of Deming and Teddy slowed as she passed Water Street, watching for pickups leaving the tavern. "Where?" she asked.

"Out past town." Tabor nodded ahead. "Right on Highway 9. Then onto Potter Road. We're about three miles down."

Down the noisy hard-pan of Highway 9 they bravely followed their headlights. A flame-eyed possum waddled across the road, disappearing into the ferns. They turned onto Potter Road.

"Tabor, this is West Purgatory. You guys have a farm?"

"All that's left is the cow."

"Ha. Tabor Morelli *milks* a cow?"

"Cut it out, cow's dry. I just feed her. Except that right now she's got interdigital dermatitis."

Teddy veered around a pothole. "Cows don't have digits."

"Foot rot. I have to put on this antibiotic that zaps the hell out of it."

On the side of the road they came to a big red rural mailbox welded onto a half-buried iron tractor wheel. "Turn here," said Tabor. "Watch out for holes."

They jounced down the two-track lane, weaving into the ferns to avoid craters. Several hundred yards down the drive, they came to a lighted farmhouse, but Tabor pointed further down the road. "Drive on back to the barn. I've got to give the cow her medicine."

Teddy drove past the house and pulled up to the weathered barn door. "You want me to wait for you?"

Tabor jumped out. "No. Just go on up to the house and introduce yourself. Margaret'll probably put on tea."

"Tabor, I can't. I *teach* in the morning." Then, remembering, "And I've got an interview in the afternoon."

"Just hop out and say hello. And don't try to lift the barbell. I'll get it."

Teddy turned and drove back to the house, parking next to the kitchen steps. Opening the rear of the wagon, she dragged the barbell toward the tailgate and lifted it in the crook of her arms. Clumsily mounting the stairs, she climbed them one by one, calling to the lighted kitchen door. "Hello?"

Up on the stoop, she thumped the curtained door with the tip of the barbell. "Hello?" she called again. The door swung open and Teddy walked in. Dropping the barbell, she screamed as if torn from the earth.

On the white vinyl, in rich pools of blood, a woman lay looking stone-eyed at the ceiling.

2

"Tabor! Tabor!" Teddy screamed. Then she remembered that the woman might not be dead. Dropping to her knees, she felt for a pulse, numbing at the sight of the neck: fleshy slashes curling back to reveal yellow fat, purple muscle, pearly ligament. On the floor blood congealed in raspberry lakes.

Probing the throat, she pressed in several places but couldn't find the vein. "Tabor! Tabor!"

Out in the dining room a phone had fallen to the floor. Teddy crawled over and found the receiver, punching the numbers 911. Immediately an operator answered.

"There's a dead woman here." Teddy's breath came in spasms. "I'm at a house on Potter Road out past Deming."

"What is your house number, please?"

"I don't know. It's three miles outside of town and there's an iron wheel holding up the mailbox, from an old wagon."

"Don't hang up."

Teddy glanced again at the body. Now there were two long smears of blood across the vinyl following her into the dining room. The knees of her gabardine slacks were capped in brown ooze.

"What's your name, please?" asked the dispatcher.

"Teddy Morelli. How long 'til you get here?"

"Does the victim require first aid?"

"She's dead! Somebody cut her arteries."

There was a short silence and the dispatcher said, "Your house number is 3180 Potter. The patrol unit for Deming will be there in seven minutes and the ambulance will be another twenty. Don't hang up."

"I w-won't." Still on her knees, she cradled the receiver and looked around. The dining room was chaos. Across the rag rug computer paper splayed like an accordion. On the desk the terminal screen was a spiderweb of cracked glass. Underneath it, the black panel of the hard-drive had been wrenched out, baring the circuits within.

Footsteps sounded on the back porch stairs.

"Tabor, don't come in!"

Out from the kitchen came a heart-rending bellow, the sound of a calf being led to slaughter. Tabor fell to her knees and picked up the dead woman by the shoulders. "Margaret!"

"Is everything all right?" asked the dispatcher.

Teddy sobbed. "I'm sorry, I can't stay on the phone anymore."

"No, wait . . ."

Without hanging up, Teddy laid the receiver down and crawled back out to Tabor. "Don't look at her, Tabor. Don't touch."

Tabor gaped at the sinewy slashes and bolted to her feet. Sucking air, she wheezed loudly, desperately trying to fill her lungs. Eyes panicky, she inhaled like a suction toy, and turned to Teddy for help.

"Tabor, stop. You're hyperventilating." Teddy looked around the kitchen.

On the pantry shelf lay a box of plastic bags. Teddy leaped over Margaret's body and pulled out a quart-size baggie, peeling it open for Tabor. "Here. Breathe in this."

Tabor blew into the plastic, then collapsed it with a breath. In and out, in and out, she bellowed and collapsed the bag as silvery condensation beaded the inside walls. After a dozen breaths she yanked it off and coolly handed it to Teddy. "I'm leaving."

"Tabor, you can't! The police are coming." Teddy grabbed her sister's arm.

"Fuck the police." Tabor wrestled free.

"Stop!" Teddy ran over and barred the door with her body. "You can't leave yet."

"I can't breathe!"

Far down the driveway came the moan of a siren. Teddy and Tabor stared fearfully into one another's eyes. The whine grew insistent and in a moment red and blue flashes of light pulsed through the woods. Soberly they hugged, staring again at the glistening pool under Margaret. Making their way to the front door, they waited for the sheriff, suddenly realizing that the longest part of the night was still ahead.

Next noon, under the campus bus shelter, a tiny flutist played a melancholy phrase. She was having trouble with the grace notes and couldn't master their time. Teddy turned up the collar of her brown velvet trenchcoat and stared at the sumptuous purple lining of the flute case. She thought about grace notes, and rainy November days.

In a minute Tabor's blue Mazda pulled up to the bus stop and Teddy dashed through the drizzle to climb in. Glancing over, Teddy examined her sister to see how she had weathered the night.

"Well?" asked Tabor. "Do I look like a breeder?"

"You look fine."

Still wet from the shower, Tabor had attempted to comb down her damp black ringlets into a sedate "breeder girl" hairdo. She wore new teal sweats with purple stripes, and Nikes with a teal-colored swoosh. On the console was her sole accessory, a teal and purple water bottle. Teddy turned away, relieved: outfit coordination seemed a sign of mental health. "You get any sleep last night?"

Tabor wheeled left onto Holly Street. "Hell, no. I laid there waiting for you to come in and get mental on me."

"Me?"

Tabor swatted the gear shift. "I guess you don't realize what your face looked like when you found her. I didn't even recognize you."

Teddy glanced into the outside mirror. Her brown bob was shiny and intact. Her eyes dark and round, revealing nothing. "I was okay. Just. Frozen. What are you going to say to the police?"

"Who cares?"

"Do they *know*?"

"Yeah. I did dyke for what's-his-name. He picked it up right away."

"Lieutenant Russell." Teddy turned again to look at Tabor. "That's not going to be a problem, is it? We can always swing by the Women's Alliance and get somebody to come with us."

Tabor shook her head. "Naw, he's on the program. Matter of fact, he's really sucking up to me. It'd be kinda fun, if it wasn't so awful."

Teddy tendered cautiously, "When you said Margaret was fifty-five I just assumed you guys, ah, weren't—"

Tabor snapped, "Why is it that everyone thinks that all lesbians do is fuck each other?"

Teddy bit her lip.

Softening, Tabor stretched her fingers isometrically on the steering wheel, barely controlling the car. "Maybe we were coming to that. She was really shy about her body." In silence she parked next to the sheriff's yellow curb and climbed out, grabbing her matching water bottle.

Teddy grimaced, wanting her sister perfect and unimpeachable for the interview. "Tabor, you can't bring that into the sheriff's office. This is the real world."

"Oh." Tabor threw it back in the car.

"And if he gives you any grief at all, we're getting you a lawyer."

Tabor trotted up the walk. "Watch out, folks. She's a feisty one."

The sheriff's office was decorated like an upscale dentist's office with mauve carpet and a groomed receptionist behind an oak and Formica counter.

"We're here to see Lieutenant Russell."

"Oh, yes." The receptionist flashed sympathy as she rose. "He's waiting for you."

She led them down the hall and left them alone in a generic conference room with a cafeteria table and molded plastic chairs. Immediately in the doorway appeared Lieutenant Russell, the deputy with the Kentucky accent and sandy mustache who had so kindly taken their stories the night before.

Dressed more formally today in chinos and an oxford shirt, Lieutenant Russell carried a legal pad, two pens, and a dark green water bottle from the Seattle Marathon. Arranging his things like a place setting on the table, he blitzed the women with his sandy smile.

"Ladies, good morning, or rather good afternoon. Can I get you anything to eat? A bagel?"

Tabor plopped into a chair. "No, thank you. I just had breakfast."

"I've already eaten," said Teddy. Tactfully she glanced up at the wall clock. "And I still have my appointment at two o'clock. I have to leave at one."

Russell looked up too. "Oh, yes. Thank you for reminding me. We need to keep on task here." Pulling out a chair, he eased himself down, sipping from the water bottle and aligning his pens with the notepad. "Well, I was very happy to find that your stories correlated so nicely last night; you both seem like such lovely people." He lifted an eyebrow engagingly. "Of course that leaves us with the knotty inconvenience of needing to look for suspects now."

Before they could respond, he continued. "But first things first . . ."

From under his legal pad he pulled a manila envelope and shook out a worn black leather address book. "The mounties just called back. They talked to Ms. Zimmerman's sister on Vancouver Island and are now asking us if there is someone else who might take next-of-kin responsibilities."

Tabor stared at Margaret's address book, intimate and out of place. "What's wrong with her sister?"

Russell shrugged. "I got the impression that the woman wasn't entirely—" he chose a word "—reliable."

"Oh."

"This sister, she's the only relative?" He prodded the address book towards Tabor with his pencil eraser, as if it were hot to the touch. "No children, anything like that?"

Tabor shook her head. "She was married once a long time ago, but they didn't—She doesn't think she was fertile."

"In any case, this sister—" Russell referred to his legal pad. "March Hunt—relayed the information that she would like to talk to someone down here who knew Margaret and we said we would kindly ask you to make that call."

Tabor shrugged. "No problem. I'd be glad to."

"Very good." Russell bounced his pen on the soft yellow pad. "Okay, then ladies, let's see if we can't tear the bone out of the big one here. We scenarioed a hate crime," he nodded respectfully to Tabor, "but at this point we can't make it fit." He answered Teddy's furrowed query. "No graffiti, no ugliness.

"Which is not to say," he continued, "that we won't be making inquiries. Nor will we pass over your list of people who knew her from the Women's Alliance.

"But," he touched his notes, "because everything in the

kitchen last night was so clean, what I'd like to focus on today is Ms. Zimmerman's computer."

Audibly Tabor gasped at his offhand dismissal of Margaret's violent death.

He smiled to coax her onward. "Oh, I'm sorry. What I mean is, the kitchen reads like a real clean . . . first-degree murder. Premeditated, but why? What we don't understand is that mess out there in the living room. I suppose y'all both saw that?"

Teddy tugged the flaps of her tweed blazer around to warm her sides. "All I remember was a smashed VDT screen."

"Not only the screen. Somebody tried to open the hard-drive like an underwear drawer. Damnedest thing. In addition, we couldn't find any of her disks and assume they must have all been taken. Now, why do y'all suppose someone would take her disks?"

Keen-eyed, Tabor leaned forward, warming to his idea. "But she wrote *children's* books. I can't imagine anyone being threatened by that."

"Do you know any of the people who came to visit her?"

"Nobody did."

"Nobody? Think hard."

Tabor shrugged. "She *was* interviewing the neighbor lady, but that was months ago."

"And what was that about?"

Tabor blinked. "Margaret never talked about her work."

"She had *no* regular visitors? No one dropping off packages, things like that?"

"Packages?" Tabor was thoroughly confused.

Teddy broke in, "He's asking about drugs, Tabor. Did she sell drugs?"

"You've got to be kidding."

Russell stroked his mustache. "But you don't know how she supported herself?"

"Savings?" Tabor said. "She was very frugal."

"We'll look into it." Russell scribbled a note and leaned his chair back on two legs, reviewing his list of questions.

"I hope you weren't shocked that we considered you girls suspects, but we are assuming the killer is somebody she knew."

"I wouldn't." Tabor shook her head. "We always leave the doors unlocked."

"Yes." Russell nodded. "We saw that. But what we also noticed was the killer's approach. As far as we can tell, all he—or she—did was just wait between the refrigerator and the dining room door, then step out and slash Ms. Zimmerman's throat from behind. Twice, no less. And unless the autopsy turns up a concussive head wound, we tend to think that rather remarkable: close, confined, very clean. She didn't even *try* to run away."

"Then you must not know about her hip," said Tabor.

"Her hip?"

"She had osteoarthritis and walked with a limp. Some screwed-up hip operation in Seattle."

"When was that?"

"Five years ago. It wasn't getting any better. I told her to sue. This is America, not Canada."

Russell snapped to attention. "Did she?"

"I don't know. She didn't tell me very much," Tabor added wistfully.

Sympathetically Russell bestowed his best professional positive regard. Glancing at his list, he said, "Well, then, ladies, let's go through the drill one more time, see if we can't find the squeaky shoe." Starting at the top, he began, "Do you remember any vehicles on Potter Road as you were driving in?"

"No," they said in tandem.

"Did you see any unusual or suspicious activity in the town of Deming as you drove through?"

"No," they echoed again.

"Did you see any unusual or suspicious activity anytime on the Mount Baker Highway?"

They responded to his litany with negatives, then, under his amiable Southern probing, recounted for the fourth time the events of the night before. Teddy told how she crawled to the phone to dial 911. Tabor, in a voice taut enough to launch arrows, retold how she bounded up the kitchen steps to find Margaret in a bloody pool with chalk-white Teddy kneeling by the phone. They both recounted their wait in the kitchen for the sheriff's car, the ambulance, then the other personnel, including Russell himself.

Several times he rephrased their testimony mistakenly and they had to correct him. When it became apparent that this was to test their telling of the story, Russell fell back to questioning, trying to jog Tabor's recent memory of Margaret's phone calls and mail.

In a while Teddy peeked at her watch. Russell noticed, and glanced at the clock, pushing his chair back and stretching. "Well, ladies, it doesn't look like we were able to stir anything up today. But thank you for coming. Ms. Morelli, I know you need to get down to the other end of the lake. Do you want a ride?"

Teddy reached for her purse. "No, thank you. Tabor—oh, you're staying for the phone call, aren't you?"

Tabor nodded somberly.

"Then I will need a ride—to my office, Lieutenant. My tape recorder's there."

Russell scooped up his legal pad and escorted them out into the hall. "I'm surprised you don't use a video camera for interviews. I thought everybody did these days."

"Then it would take two people. Audio works fine, all we need is his voice."

"Which reminds me." Russell stretched, cuddling his yellow pad like a stuffed animal. "How is it that somebody like Walter Lloyd ends up speaking an Indian language anyway? Was he raised by Lummis?"

"Oh, no." Teddy shook her head. "Chinook's not an Indian language. It's the old trade jargon used by both Indians and whites all up and down the coast until about eighty years ago. Walter Lloyd is the last fluent Chinook speaker—in the world, as far as we can tell." She made her way emphatically to the door. "I appreciate your working around my interview. When his nurse said he was going in for routine surgery Monday, we knew we'd better get it done."

"Well, if you can do it, we can do it."

At the reception area she reached a hand out to the door. She leveled her gaze on Tabor and asked, "Are you okay?" She checked Tabor's eyes for stress, for a lie, for anything.

Deep in Tabor's brown eyes was a strange glimmer.

"What?"

Tabor whispered, madly. "Her sister on Vancouver Island is going to know about the people in her books."

Teddy looked at Russell, alarmed. Russell touched Tabor on the arm, then took in Teddy too. "Which reminds me, I have one more bit of messiness to annoy you girls with. Last night, while you were waiting for the aid car to arrive, did either of you accidentally move or dispose of the murder weapon?"

They blinked with surprise.

"What we are looking for, of course, is a very sharp knife, or maybe a scalpel."

"No. Nothing like that."

"A scalpel," repeated Teddy.

"Well," he said, "it was worth a try. Let me know if you remember something." The deputy extended a hand to Teddy. "In any case, have a pleasant afternoon, Professor Morelli. I'll send somebody around to take you up to campus."

She scurried into the lobby.

"Oh, by the way, Professor."

She turned, patiently feigning attention.

"We'll be in contact," he continued. "So, if you please, for the next little while, could you not leave town, or at least keep us posted on your whereabouts?"

3

Nigel was there; she could smell the moth-balls.

Reconnoitering around the corner of the history office, Teddy waited until she heard him inside collecting his mail. Tiptoeing past the mailroom, she sprinted down the hall and dashed into her office, noiselessly closing the door.

Thump, thump, thump, came the rap on her door. "Teddy? It's me, Nigel."

Grabbing the phone receiver, she pressed it to her shoulder like a burping baby. "Come in!" she called. She talked to the droning receiver: "Someone's just come in, excuse me a moment."

"Nigel, what is it?"

Tiny Nigel Czerny slipped off his glasses and coyly dropped them in the pocket of his superbly tailored little sports coat. It was Nigel's custom tweeds that smelled of mothballs. Nobody had the heart to tell him.

"First editions," Nigel beamed. He glowed as brightly as his polished forehead. "Seventeenth and eighteenth century."

"I'm on the phone, Nigel."

"I can see." Jauntily he turned on his heel. "I'll bring them down in a minute." He wriggled his fingers goodbye.

"Damn." Teddy slammed the receiver and climbed on

24

a chair, still wrapped in her brown velvet coat. Dragging down the tape recorder and a handful of cassettes, she ripped the cellophane from the tapes and spun them quickly fast-forward to tighten them for the interview. She spread the mouth of her book satchel, and packed in headphones, extension cords, and the brittle yellow Chinook dictionary on special loan from the Rare Book Room of the library.

There was a knock on her door. A radiant, white-gloved Nigel appeared, reverently offering two books. One was an ancient maroon half-Morocco with gilt bands and marbled edges. The other was a primitive tan calfskin—almost medieval looking—that on second glance had been rebound last century in someone's private library.

"Oh, Nigel. They're beautiful. I'd really like to look, but not now. You wouldn't believe how horrible the last twenty-four hours have been. My sister and I had a grisly experience last night and I haven't had any sleep. Now I've got to go tape somebody at the south end of Lake Whatcom." She threw the cassettes in her satchel. "I don't even have time to tell you about it."

"Oh, we've all heard, love. You and Tabor were the ones who found that Canadian woman. I actually brought the books in to cheer you up: *les belles choses que ne changent—pas.*"

"Nigel." She softened. "Thank you so much, but I really do have to be at the far end of Lake Whatcom in forty minutes."

He looked at his watch. "Plenty of time. Just a peek." He proffered the home-bound calfskin volume.

Cradling the heavy volume in her ungloved hand, she opened it only wide enough to read the pages, as Nigel had taught her. Inside, the leaves were creamy vellum. From the frontispiece Teddy read aloud.

" 'The History of France, written in Italian by the Count Priorato, containing all the memorable actions in France and other neighboring kingdoms. Translated by the Right

Honorable Henry, late Earl of Monmouth, Grays-Inne. London, MDCLXXVI.' 1676,'' she deciphered. "What 'memorable actions' are they talking about?"

"The Fronde—1648—when the nobles tried to loosen things up under Louis XIV's regent, Cardinal Marzipan."

"Mazarin," she corrected.

He cocked an eyebrow at her, to indicate he had made a joke.

Grinning, she reached for the other volume.

" '*Troisieme voyage de Captaine Cook, ou Voyage à l'Ocean Pacifique*.' Oh, Nigel! I want to look at this."

"I knew you would."

"So." She caressed the marbled edges. "It's been translated for the French market. What century?" She counted the Roman "C's" and "X's" on the next page. "1785. That's immediately after Cook's third voyage. I had no idea there was such a demand for Cook on the continent."

"Sure." He stood too close, emphasizing their shared height—soulmates, as it were. "Figure it was the eighteenth-century equivalent of space exploration. They needed Cook's journals to find out what to exploit next. I know you have to run now, but let's have another go at it at dinner Saturday night, I make a wonderful Crab Mornay. Have you ever eaten it over," he narrowed his eyes seductively, "toast points?"

"Toast points?" She snapped her book satchel. "You Europeanists are so decadent."

He blocked the door. "Cheerios. We'll eat Cheerios, we'll read to each other from back of the box."

"Nigel," she pleaded. She looked at his feet, getting ready to fake towards the door.

Casually, he leaned against the oak slab, cradling his volumes. "Has anyone ever told you you look like a little chocolate truffle in that brown velvet coat?"

Teddy stiffened. "No. I don't think so." She grabbed

the handles of her book satchel. "Nigel, I really have to go. I'm late."

"Sunday afternoon?" he asked.

"Look, Nigel." She didn't know what to say. "I'm sorry. No, okay?"

His eyes flashed pain. "Well then, no problem, I understand perfectly." Straightening his back, he turned and walked away.

"Nigel!"

He closed his office door.

Outside Teddy dashed across the red brick square through the afternoon mist. Flinging her book satchel onto the car seat, she placed the tape recorder on the floor. She maneuvered the Subaru from the faculty lot and headed east to the lake.

There were no cars at mid-afternoon and the wet asphalt glowed mother-of-pearl in the fragile winter light. Veering right at the Lakeway divide, she passed the turnoff to her own condo on the north shore. She ignored the center line except at curves, and watched enviously as the windsurfers on the lake skimmed through postcard vistas. Driving out past the fine houses on the point, she steered lazily, glancing at the tiny cusp beaches and mossy rotting docks.

Finally, just before the gate announcing Forest Service lands, the road turned inland and Teddy briefly lost sight of the lake. Braking the car, she spotted the granite marker she had been told to look for on the left. She rolled up to the pillar to read, testing the syllables carved in stone: "*Saghalie Illahee.*" Pulling out her Chinook dictionary, she looked up the words. *Saghalie* meant "high." *Illahee* was "place, ground, meadow, or home."

"High ground," she said, to no one in particular.

Steering down the dirt drive, she got her first glimpse of the log house on the high rise in front of her. Like a half-size copy of Yellowstone Lodge, it was rough-hewn of whole tree trunks, with dormered roofs and profuse chimneys.

Following the winding drive through a forest of towering rhododendrons, she took the sandstone rise back up to high ground. Rounding the curve, she pulled into the graveled kitchen lot behind the great two-story house.

Teddy decided she should probably use the main door and, tugging her book satchel and tape recorder from the car, walked around to the shallow front yard to look out on the wintery lake. Down the sheer cliff a stairway led to a shingle beach and sturdy dock. At the far end of the dock was a glassed-in gazebo with its own cast-iron firepit.

Turning to the house, Teddy looked down the ninety-foot length of front veranda. Four great bays with mullioned casements and built-in window seats jutted out at regular intervals. Inside against the glass lay faded maroon pillows, gray on the back from years in the sun. Wind rustled the trees, pelting her head with droplets. She hurried onto the porch.

Thumping the blackened knocker, Teddy was greeted quickly by a nurse in a zippered smock. She had short black hair molded into perfect waves, and a similarly managed smile. "Come in," she said, not meaning it at all. "I'm Mrs. Dykstra. Mr. Lloyd's been expecting you."

Teddy stepped into the low-ceilinged entry and looked into the great room beyond. Out in the center was a massive fireplace of ferrous stone rising two stories to the planked roof. At the far end, the ceiling lowered again for the dining area, where an immense wrought-iron chandelier hung over the table like an instrument of medieval torture. All the interior walls were logs stacked to the ceiling like fat golden crayons and everywhere hung maps and tapestries. Teddy walked into the vast room and let her eyes follow the craggy chimney to the ceiling.

The nurse interrupted. "Won't you have a seat?" She pointed to a faded couch carved with stags and dogs.

Teddy sat. "Thank you." Springs in the sofa rose up to greet her.

"Are you one of the Morellis from the news this morning?"

"Oh. I guess we're notorious now." Discreetly she searched for a more compatible seat.

"Margaret Zimmerman was my neighbor. I live in Deming."

"Really? I keep forgetting how small the county is."

"I sent my husband over with cinnamon rolls, but the sheriff had it all blocked off."

"I guess he would."

The nurse turned. "I'll see if Mr. Lloyd's ready." Crossing to the far end of the room, she disappeared up a rough-hewn stairway.

Instantly Teddy hopped from the couch and looked around. Outside, a rogue wind rattled the storm glass and blue rain poured in earnest. Inside the silence was chin deep. Next to the sofa, under a glass dome, four brass balls whirled silently in an air clock, like a pinwheel catching light. They stopped slowly, then spun in the opposite direction.

In a moment Mrs. Dykstra appeared on the stairs. "He can see you now."

Teddy gathered her things and followed the nurse up the broad steps. Against the stair rail a hydraulic wheelchair lift had been installed and Mrs. Dykstra said, "You know, he had a stroke in May."

"They told me that. He sounded okay on the phone."

"Oh, he never lost language functions, it was a right hemisphere infarct. Partially paralyzed on his left. He had a bad night last night so we decided he could see you only if he stayed in bed. I'm hoping you won't stay too long."

"Of course not."

They passed half a dozen mahogany doors on which were mounted small brass plaques. At the end of the hall the nurse knocked once, then swung open the door. Across the room cathedral-sized windows opened out to a balcony and a panoramic view of the lake. Teddy glanced out at the navy hills and mushroom-shaped Reveille Island. She turned. Behind her lay a pale balding man in a hospital bed. Smiling, she pointed outside to the cloud-soaked mountains. "*Saghalie Illahee.*"

Walter Lloyd beamed. "That's right. 'High place.' That makes you the first person in years who won't be asking me about the name of my house."

The nurse left, closing the door behind her.

Walking over to admire the view, Teddy watched droplets collect in the leadwork of each diamond pane. "Your house is wonderful. How old is it?"

Lloyd adjusted his withered left arm, pretending to be casual. He had a shiny, well-shaped head and pink baggy pockets under his eyes. Although bedridden, he had the air of a man with no time to waste. "My father built this house at the end of the Depression. We'd just been to Mount Hood and admired the lodge going up there. Came back here and built one just like it. Certainly doesn't seem like sixty years ago."

Teddy set her satchel on a table placed beside the bed. "Time does go fast, doesn't it?"

"Bah." Lloyd jerked his right leg in annoyance. "How would you know? You couldn't be a day over thirty."

"Thank you. Thirty-three."

"Not married, are you?"

Teddy flinched. "Not yet."

"Funny how you can tell. You career girls don't seem to be in a hurry these days."

Unwinding the extension cord, she plugged it into the wall. "I can't speak for *other* career girls, but all I know is that when you're my age all the good men have long been taken." Teddy parted her fingers in the "Star Trek" salute. "Last guy I dated was a psychologist who goes to sci-fi conventions as a Klingon."

Lloyd laughed and sputtered, ending up in a coughing spasm.

"Oh, dear. I got you excited."

"No. No problem." He coughed again. "Now, what'd you say your name was?"

"Teddy Morelli."

"Teddy? Well, Teddy, I hear they're not going to give us much time, so we better get started. You wawa any Chinook?"

She held up her thumb and forefinger to indicate an inch. "*Tenas*. Only what I got from the dictionary."

"The *snass* getting you down?"

"Time out. You're already over my head." She took out the brittle dictionary and riffled pages. " '*Snass*: rain.' Yes, I'm tired of the *snass*. It's growing mold on my bathroom walls." She began to arrange her things on the table.

"Which dictionary is that?"

"Gill's, 1909."

"I don't know that one. May I?"

She handed him the faded little pamphlet. "J.K. Gill, from Portland. They're a chain now."

"Oh, yes." Pressing the book against his thigh, he turned pages awkwardly from the top. Reading out loud, he recited, " '*La-shandell*, a candle; *lapote*, a door'—what peculiar spelling. " '*La-shase*, a chair.' You know what language those words are from?"

"Sure, that's French, that's what the trappers added."

"Whole passel of nouns from the French, all begin with 'L.' " He read again: " '*Lamontay*, a mountain; *lasheminay*, a chimney.' No, I don't like this spelling at all. You should get the Shaw dictionary, that's the one that cleans up all that. I'll let you borrow mine. Shaw used ten other sources before—"

"Wait! Don't start yet. I need to turn on the tape recorder

so we won't lose any of this." Teddy popped a tape into the recorder, then held up the tie-clip microphone and pinched it open, staring at the shawl collar of Lloyd's pajamas. "Where should we clip this?"

Self-consciously Lloyd raised his chin as she clipped on the mike. "Now I feel like an electrical appliance." He moved his arm to the side. "Well, dang it. I can't think of anything to say."

"Don't worry. That's my job." Teddy sat next to the table and clamped earphones and a microphone on herself. Poised over the "record" buttons, she held up a finger for silence, then turned it on, waiting for a few loops of tape. Then, in a calm low voice, she began, "This is Teodora Morelli talking to Walter Lloyd about the Chinook trade jargon. We're in the bedroom of his home, *Saghalie Illahee*, looking out at Stewart Mountain across Lake Whatcom. It's early afternoon, Thursday, November sixth, and, as usual, it's raining." Turning to Lloyd, she said, "Mr. Lloyd, before we start talking about Chinook, I was wondering if you could give a little background on yourself. Do you mind telling me when and where you were born?"

Stentorian and self-conscious, Lloyd began. "I was born April 13, 1923 in Maple Falls, Washington in the bedroom of my parents' home. My father ran a lumber mill out there."

"Did you also grow up in Maple Falls?"

"That is correct. My father held the directorship of Lloyd Lumber Company for thirty-seven years. Upon his retirement in 1953 he turned it over to me."

"Your father's name was?"

He relaxed under the easy questions. "Walter Angus Lloyd. I'm Walter MacFarlane Lloyd, after my mother's family."

"Mr. Lloyd, if we go back to the absolute earliest period of your life, what's the *very* first thing you can remember?"

"The very first." Lloyd's eyes clouded with memory. "I

would say, the first thing I remember was the Fourth of July when I was three, or four—I couldn't tell you which—when my grandfather bought a brand new Pittsburgh locomotive to haul lumber out of the hills. It was about twice the size of the old lokie and Grandpa had just laid a track up to Wickersham to pull out the big cedar back there. So, on the Fourth of July they dressed up this new lokie with red, white, and blue streamers and two American flags across the headlight. Then they loaded all the families from the mill on the cars and took them out to Wickersham for a picnic. I got to ride up front with the engineer. I was so proud.''

Teddy smiled. ''That's nice. Can you recall anything else from that period?''

A shadow crossed his face. ''The next thing I remember was when my mother was sick. She had been in bed for a long time and I hardly ever got to see her. One Sunday morning I was sitting in the kitchen with Jefferson, the yardman. He was Nooksack Indian. It was after church and I still had my suit on. I was dipping bread into a glass of milk—Jefferson didn't drink milk—and I don't know what I said—something about lunch being late—and Jefferson answered, very quietly, 'T'sladie memaloose.' 'T'sladie' is what they called my mother, it's Chinook for 'lady.' I remember I wouldn't look up or say anything—I just kept dipping bread because, although no one had told me up 'til that very moment, I already knew my mother was dying.''

Teddy searched for the four-year-old child hidden in his ravaged face. ''Oh, that's awful. Is Jefferson the one who taught you Chinook?''

He exhaled deeply. ''I don't remember anyone actually teaching me Chinook, although I spoke it most often with Jefferson and Jesse, his son. Jesse was exactly my age and the only other child out in Maple Falls at the time. We used Chinook as our play language.'' Looking at the sheet draped over his legs, Lloyd added, "Jesse died last spring. That really threw me for a loop."

"I'm so sorry. It must have been a terrible blow." Turning up the volume incrementally, she said, "You know, I think the best thing we could do today is get you to speak as much Chinook as possible. Everything you can think of."

"Fine. What would you like me to say?"

"For starters, why were the bunch of you out in Maple Falls speaking Chinook well into the 1920s? When Franz Boas, the anthropologist, went looking for Chinook speakers in the 1890s, all he could find were two elderly Indian women."

Lloyd's wiry eyebrows rippled like woolly bear caterpillars. "Why didn't he try the Rainier Club in downtown Seattle?"

There was a soft knock on the door and Mrs. Dykstra came in. "Just about through?"

Lloyd growled irritably. "No, Mrs. Dykstra. We were just getting started. Weren't we, Teddy? I was going to say the Ten Commandments for her."

"It's time for your medication," pressed the nurse.

Peevishly Lloyd adjusted his withered arm. "Well, come on in."

Mrs. Dykstra scurried into the room and poured water from a pitcher on the dresser. Bringing Lloyd an amber pill vial, she wrestled off the cap and rolled two tablets into his bony hand. As he gulped water, she said, "You won't be much longer, will you?"

He put down his glass, avoiding her eyes. "I don't know. Teddy and I have a lot to talk about. Mrs. Dykstra, could you go down to the library and look for my Chinook files? They're in the desk, either in the bottom left drawer or the one above that."

"I really don't think—"

"Mrs. Dykstra, please."

The nurse left the room and Lloyd grinned like the Cheshire cat. "Now, where were we?"

"The Ten Commandments."

"Oh, yes." Lloyd's eyes glistened. "I think I know them all. If I don't, we'll do them English and translate backwards."

"I doubt I can remember them in *English*."

"Naw, we can do this. Okay, are you ready? Number one: 'I am the Lord thy God, thou shall not have strange gods before me,' or *'Nika Saghalie Tyee kopa mika. Kopit ikt mika kumtux Saghalie Tyee.'* He narrowed his eyes. "You know what *'Saghalie Tyee'* is?"

"High something."

"High chief. Literally the first commandment says, 'I am your High Chief. Stop once you know High Chief.' Number two." He wagged a finger. " *'Wake cultus wawa, Saghalie Tyee nem.'* No bad speak Saghalie Tyee's name."

Teddy smiled and looked at the brown plastic tape looping through the machine, imbedding itself with the sounds of the last speaker of one of the last maritime trade languages on earth. She nodded encouragement as he recalled that one should honor *'mika papa'* and *'mika mama,'* and leafed through her dictionary at commandment number six to learn that adultery had been translated for the indigenous people as "shame thing about your flesh."

After the commandments, Lloyd remembered a story about two children who threw clam shells at their mother and were turned into otters. The minutes passed and he told a story—half in English—of jigging for dogfish with Jesse on the Nooksack. When an hour was up Teddy changed tapes and Lloyd sang a Lummi language rowing song, and then remembered the verse Nooksacks used for greeting at potlatch. As the winter light faded over Stewart Mountain, he described his father and his mother in Chinook and then moved on to discuss its French-Nootka-Clatsop-English origins. Teddy's second tape clicked off in the middle of his explaining why "*pelton*" was Chinook for "fool" and Lloyd looked at the clock next to his bed. "I've talked for two hours."

"I don't feel like we're finished, do you?"

"Barely scratched the surface. Hope I'm not boring you."

"Not at all." Teddy stood and stretched. "I could listen forever."

"And I haven't even done the Lord's Prayer, have I? Darn it, where's Mrs. Dykstra with my files? I wanted to sing some of those old missionary hymns I have written down."

Teddy unplugged the extension cord. "Well, we need to do this again. I can't think of a nicer way to spend a rainy afternoon."

"Indeed." Lloyd sighed and slumped back into the pillows, suddenly tired. Looking out toward the navy-colored hillside, his eyes blurred with reflection. "Jesse never minded the rain. You know what he used to say?" He turned to watch her pack equipment.

"What?"

"On days like this he would hold up his finger to get you to listen and say '*wawa snass.*'"

Teddy looked at him quizzically. " '*Wawa*' is 'talk.' You told me *snass* . . .''

"Rain."

"Talk rain?"

"*Talking* rain. See? The rain was trying to tell you something, if only you'd listen."

"That's nice." Teddy wound the extension cord between her elbow and hand. "Did Jesse ever tell you what it was saying?"

Lloyd lifted his left arm and tucked it close to his thigh. "I can't remember, it's been so long ago. You know," he heaved and looked at his arm. "They said Jesse died in the wood kiln where he went to drink. But I know for a fact he had been off alcohol for at least ten years. He even helped start the AA chapter out on the reservation.''

Out in the hall someone bumped the door accidentally and Lloyd stated loudly: "Well, Teddy, I wonder if we should call Mrs. Dykstra?"

The nurse glided in. "All finished now?"

"Mrs. Dykstra, what a surprise. Teddy, what should we do about those hymns? Some of 'em are doozies."

Taking a black cuff off the wall, the nurse started rolling Lloyd's sleeve. "And I hope we haven't done any damage to your blood pressure."

"Mrs. Dykstra, I'm seventy-four years old. It doesn't matter if my blood pressure hits the Dow Jones." Craning around her bulk, he smiled at Teddy. The pink bags under his eyes puckered like little sausages. "Well then, gal, how about tomorrow? Same time? I need to go through all the material that Mrs. Dykstra forgot to bring in today."

Teddy glanced at the nurse. "Ah, I teach Friday afternoon. I can come in the morning, though."

"Splendid. I'll sing for you then."

Mrs. Dykstra plumped up Lloyd's pillows. "I don't think—"

"Of course you don't. Teddy and I are doing very valuable work. I'm sure you couldn't possibly approve." Again he leaned around the nurse's body. "Well, what do you say? I can have this place sounding like an old-fashioned Chinook revival meeting."

"Sure. That'd be great. But you know, I have a better idea. What if I leave the tape recorder and some extra tapes with you, and you sing the missionary songs tonight. That way, tomorrow we can do a grammar workup."

"What's that?"

"We go through things like syntax, declining nouns, masculine and feminine, conjugating verbs."

He waved his hand in protest. "Chinook doesn't have any of that."

Teddy handed him two hours of empty cassettes. "Then we need to indicate that, too. You're putting sentences together with some kind of logic." Smiling genially at the nurse, Teddy handed her the recorder and extension cord. "Maybe you could set this up by his bed tonight, after you're sure he's rested enough."

Pique worked the corners of Mrs. Dykstra's mouth. She took the machine.

Teddy buttoned her trenchcoat. "Is 9 a.m. a good time tomorrow?"

"Dandy." The old man's cheeks flushed. "Just dandy. And don't forget to pick up my Shaw dictionary from the office. You need to talk to Christian Wells, he's my office manager."

Teddy nodded. "Yes, he's the one who called me the first time. We discovered we live in the same condo development."

"Christian lives in a condo development at the north end of the lake."

"Y-yes." Perplexed, she turned to Mrs. Dykstra, who hovered with the blood pressure cuff. "I can let myself out."

"Could you?"

Lloyd bellowed, "Mrs. Dykstra, go see Angela to the door."

Angela? Teddy scrambled toward the hall.

The nurse dropped the cuff and led Teddy down the hall in icy silence. On the stairs the nurse said, "He's not well, you know."

"I'm sorry."

Throwing open the door, Mrs. Dykstra said, "If I call and cancel the interview tomorrow it's because his blood pressure's risen again."

"I'm sorry," repeated Teddy.

Without a word the nurse threw her out into the gray-flannel day.

4

The man in the brown leather bomber jacket worked his way across the weight room, shouting suggestions to the sweating hulks over the rock music. Tabor racked a bar above her head and wiped the smell of English Leather off the vinyl, waiting for The Bomber to come to her station. He saw he was recognized, so he gingerly walked over, adjusting the red scrapbook under his arm. "You're a hard woman to track down."

Tabor tucked the towel under her bench. "Does Teddy know you're here?"

Bomber bobbled his head, as if ducking a blow. "I wanted to talk to you first."

"Aurie, I don't think this is a good idea. Anyway, you've come at a very bad time."

Pushing his horn-rimmed glasses up his eagle nose, The Bomber smiled knowingly, eyes glowing with amusement. "For an important wrestling personality such as yourself, there really isn't a good time, is there?"

"Aurie Scholl watches wrestling?"

"You can imagine my surprise when I turned on the tube last Saturday and saw the redoubtable Tabor Morelli snarling curses at a beautiful little water sprite. Water Sprite's older than she looks, isn't she?"

39

Tabor squirted water into her mouth. "I don't tell professional secrets."

Aurie glanced around at the steroidal beefcakes hobbling like Chinese women with bound feet. "It's awfully noisy in here, can I buy you a latte someplace?"

"I don't do caffeine." She wiped her mouth. "There's a juice bar next door."

"Fine."

Slipping a tee shirt over her spandex, Tabor grabbed her belly pack and led him into the front parlor of the Kharma Juice Company where divinely inspired hippies squeezed liquid eloquence from all manner of fruits and vegetables. Climbing onto a high stool next to the window, Tabor caught the attention of the bearded clerk. "I'll have a double carrot-ginger."

Aurie frowned. "Is that good?"

Tabor called to the clerk. "He'll have a double Valencia."

The juices came and they took long draughts. "Tastes like Beverly Hills," said Aurie.

"I wouldn't know."

"Which reminds me: a cardiologist from L.A. has us all playing squash with an English ball. Whole different game. Next time you're in Seattle, I'll bring you to the club."

Wiping fog off her glass, she asked, "You still cutting on knees?"

"Five knees a day, three days a week. Between my partners and me, we did over twenty-two hundred last year."

"Wow! That's a lot of blown-out ligaments."

"Pretty much the whole Seattle market." Gesturing to her legs, Aurie asked, "So, how are yours holding up?"

"Anterior cruciates? Fine."

"No discomfort after exercise, anything like that?" He positioned the red scrapbook on the table.

"Fortunately I'm not playing basketball four hours a day

anymore. And if I keep my exercise varied, I don't even
have to think about it."

"Good girl. Did you know yours was the first two-sided
arthroscopy I ever did? Sometimes I wince when I think
about how murky optics were back then. Any chance you'd
let me go in and take another look?"

"Ha!" Tabor hid her legs under the counter. Touching
the red scrapbook, she said, "What's this?"

Aurie pushed it over. "Some of my more illustrious pa-
tients. Your part starts at the bookmark."

"May I?"

"Of course!"

Tabor opened the album and found yellowing University
of Washington Lady Husky basketball clippings under plastic. "My team! Oh, Aurie, I haven't thought about this stuff
in *so* long." Turning the page, she found the *Seattle Times*
photo of LaShanda Maxey standing midair above two Stan-
ford guards. Next to LaShanda was Tabor's own grinning
mug shot and the feature article that ran the day after she
had scored thirty-two points against the Cougars. She
scanned the aging columns of sports-page hype, the frenetic
verbs and shimmering adjectives, all cataloging that period
of time when the world treated them as beings apart, and
they had believed.

Turning the page, she found an article announcing her
knee surgery and five-week hiatus. Interspersed throughout
were confident quotes from the illustrious orthopedist, Dr.
Aurelian Scholl. "Oh, Aurie, I had forgotten all this."

She came to a picture of the team huddled anxiously
around Coach Gobrecht, a colossal Chinese flag in the
background. Nostalgia welled up in her eyes. "I remember
this. We had a great time on that trip."

"Bet you never guessed how they financed it?"

Tabor's eyes widened. "You?"

Aurie shrugged modestly. "We sent a donation from the
clinic."

"Aurie, I had no idea. Thank you."

"You're welcome. You guys were a lot of fun." He blinked wistfully and added, "As a matter of fact, you guys were the most fun I ever had."

Tabor looked up from the album. "Meaning me and my team, or me and Teddy?"

His face softened, eyes fragile as cracked amber behind the horned-rims. "How is she?"

Tabor shook her head, dark ringlets jousting for hegemony. "I don't think you ought to be doing this, Aurie. You know she hates your guts. And anyway, I already told you: you've come at a bad time."

"Sorry." Aurie turned up his palms. "Thursday's my only day off."

"That's not what I mean. It just so happens the woman I live with was murdered last night. Teddy and I found her."

"Tabor!"

Tabor nodded. "The sheriff's office is driving us crazy and Teddy isn't even taking any time off. I don't think my brain is here right now."

"Tabor, this is highly traumatic. Do you want to talk about it?"

"Not right now." She clutched her juice glass. "I don't even know how I *feel*, much less how to talk about it."

"I'd really like to help."

"Go back to Seattle, Aurie."

"But I just found you." He looked at his watch. "Want to go do something? Can I take you out?"

"Can't." She slid off the stool. "I'm supposed to meet a man about our cow." She waved her hand in frustration. "Please don't make me explain, it's too complicated."

"Wait, wait." He rushed dramatically to block her exit. "Aurelian Scholl is not so easily deterred. How about dinner tonight? Tabor Morelli was always a zealous trencherwoman as I remember."

Tabor honed in like a bird dog on quarry. "What did you have in mind?"

"How's the Lebanese restaurant on the way into town?"

"Seriously good."

"What if I meet you there about six?"

"You're paying, I'll be there."

"Excellent. See you at six."

Kicking off her brown wingtip oxfords, Teddy punched "playback" on the answering machine and collapsed on the couch.

"Hello, Teddy?" It was Nigel. "I'm just now looking at the appendices in the Cook volume and I found a Nootka-French glossary. It's really a kick. I'm going out in a while, should I bring it by?"

"Oh, Nigel." She pulled a cushion over her head and the machine beeped again. "Hello, this is your neighbor, Christian Wells. I just opened the *Tribune* and saw what happened last night. I'm really sorry, I hope you're okay. I guess since you didn't interview Mr. Lloyd today, we need to talk about setting up another appointment when things settle down for you." He paused. "Although, of course, we really shouldn't put it off too long."

"The *Tribune*," Teddy moaned. Slipping on her shoes, she pushed back the glass patio door, inhaling the chill off the lake. Silver fog hovered around the porch lights while down at the dock canoes rumbled despondently. Picking her way over paving stones, she kept her eyes straight ahead, unwilling to violate her neighbors' fragile privacy.

She arrived at Christian Wells's condo and thumped on the glass door, looking in. Covering his dining room wall was an eccentric mural of fantastically drawn gourmands in lurid colors. All had their mouths open.

No one answered her knock and she heard music from the study off the front entry. Knocking louder, she waited, and out of the study came Christian, confused that someone had knocked on his patio door. Teddy blinked and caught her breath: it was *he*, the beautiful windsurfer who looked like a Nordstrom's model.

Opening the glass awkwardly with his elbow, Christian smiled. "You're Teddy. Come in."

She kept her eyes off his toned body. "And you're one of the windsurfers. I've actually almost talked to you a couple of times. It looks like so much fun."

"Next best thing to flying." He had an agreeably long face with chiseled cheekbones and a wicked jaw. A curly shock of sunstreaked hair tumbled over his forehead, and his green eyes were the color of Douglas fir. But he looked awfully young.

Teddy slid the door closed behind her. "Am I interrupting something?" In the background Mozart soared in barely controlled arpeggios and the warm air smelled of roasting chicken. Christian held his hands aloof, careful not to touch anything.

"You're not interrupting anything. I've just got glue drying."

"You'll be happy to know I did interview Mr. Lloyd this afternoon. It went swimmingly well."

"You're kidding?" His eyes shone appraisingly. "You must have nerves of steel."

"Or else I'm plain stupid. I'm going to be a basket case when it finally hits me." She exhaled. "But actually what I came down for is to ask to see your *Tribune*. I don't get it at home."

Christian gestured toward the living room. "On the coffee table. Can you get it? I need to get back to my glue."

"I *am* interrupting."

"No, no." He waved her back towards the study. "Bring the paper with you. I'd love company."

Teddy picked up the *Tribune*, noticing the dramatic black and white herringbone inlay of the wood table top. Walking back to the study, she read the headline out loud,

" 'COUNTY WOMAN BRUTALLY SLAIN.' " She scanned the information, all of which she already knew, and stopped at the study door. Christian had the room set up as a woodshop with wall-to-wall countertops, plastic runners over the carpet, and a jigsaw in the corner.

She folded the *Tribune* into a stiff column and perched on the edge of a stool. "Here we are. 'Zimmerman's body was discovered at 10:13 by housemate, Tabor Morelli, 32, and Dr. Theodora Morelli, 33, assistant professor at Western University.' Great. They're going to love this in my department."

Christian sandwiched thin rounds of wood onto coaster-sized circles of plywood. Centering them deftly, he immediately secured them with clamps. "How did *you* know Margaret Zimmerman?" Up close he smelled soapy and faintly male. Teddy took a deep breath.

"I didn't. My sister lives there. Or lived there. She's staying with me until she finds another place."

"Is your sister the one lifting weights in your living room this morning?"

"Damn it. I told her not to."

"And 'brutally slain.' What does that mean?"

Teddy closed her eyes. "It means somebody slashed her arteries. She bled to death."

"Gruesome."

"No. I can't describe it."

"Then that makes me all the more impressed that you made it out to Mr. Lloyd's this afternoon."

"Actually, I think that's the way academics cope: just keep plowing through." Teddy chewed her lip. "We're going to do a couple more hours tomorrow."

"Wow, thank you. You have no idea how much this means to him." Christian placed the drying coasters at the back of the workbench and began cutting two-inch squares of gleaming satinwood with an X-acto knife.

Teddy looked around the shop. Strewn about were exquisitely colored pieces of paper-thin woods. Colors ranged from near-white to russet and ebony. Leaning against the wall was a striking circular tabletop: a starburst compass rose inlaid with burgundy, mustard, and beige. Next to the window was an unvarnished jewel case in walnut, maple, and teak.

"You do inlay," she said.

"It's called marquetry. I hope you don't mind if I keep working. I need to finish this chessboard before Christmas."

"The woods are really beautiful."

He looked up appreciatively, his eyes like forest shade. "They are, aren't they?"

This time she barely blinked. "Did you make the coffee table in the living room?" She watched his hands as he worked. They were long and fine and he used them deftly, like someone who had spent years at the piano.

"The coffee table was one of my first projects. I'm much better now."

"Looks good to me."

"Thank you. The joins could be better."

"Oh, I almost forgot," she said. "Mr. Lloyd said I should ask you for his George Shaw Chinook dictionary. It's at the office."

"Sure. I know that one. Want me to drop it off?"

"That'd be great. Thank you." Seeing no place to put the *Tribune*, Teddy noticed a table in the hall next to the front door. She stepped out to lay the paper on it and saw some letters on the floor. Bending over to pick them up, she was dumbfounded to find them painted onto the wood.

"Wow! What's this?"

It was a perfect reproduction of limp blue airmail sheets, a Miami postcard, and an electric bill from Puget Sound Energy, all painted in bright acrylics and sealed under floor lacquer.

"Art." Christian looked up. "My wife was going

through her *trompe l'oeil* stage. You should go take a look at the powder room.''

Because Christian's condo was identical to her own, Teddy knew to open the door under the stairs. She pushed it back and found herself looking down the assembly line of the Kohler Porcelain Works: beige sinks and toilets—identical to the ones plumbed to the floor—reproduced to vanishing infinity on the wall. Hovering over the porcelains were plump, cheery workers in blue overalls and red neckerchiefs. Teddy laughed and went back to the study.

"I didn't know you were married," she said. "I've never seen your wife."

Christian frowned, deftly trimming a ragged corner of satinwood. "That's because Jana walked out two years ago and I haven't seen her since."

"You're kidding? But you're still married?"

The line of his jaw worked microscopically as he stared at his work. "Legally, yes. But mostly I'm just waiting for her to show up one day and make it official."

"Where is she?"

"Well." He raised his eyebrows ironically. "First she went to Nepal for spiritual enlightenment. Then she was bumming around the Great Barrier Reef scuba diving. But, last time I heard, she was in San Francisco doing performance art. She's exploring the relationship between gender equality and environmental destruction."

"Oh, I'm so sorry."

He concentrated on the ivory wood. "It's okay. On some level, I knew from the word 'go' I couldn't make her happy. And when we had to move to Bellingham, she took one look at the art scene and split."

"She *is* very talented. The mural in the dining room is an entirely different style."

"Oh, that's not hers. That's my baby brother's, Eric. He comes up here to mooch when he can't find a real job in Seattle."

"Very powerful, sort of assaults you."

"Then you should go up and see the wall in the bedroom: 'Last Supper with Naked Dwarfs.' Which is what I *wouldn't* let him do in my dining room."

Teddy burst out laughing. "I think I'll pass on that."

"Good choice. It's not for the faint-hearted. Although," he leafed through layers of sandpaper, choosing a fine black sheet with a surface like velvet, "last weekend Eric brought up a photographer who thinks 'Last Supper' is the greatest thing he's seen outside London. He wants to shoot a spread for *Northwest Design*."

"Are you going to let him?"

He shrugged. "Don't know. We—I mean, Eric—has moved onto bronze and isn't particularly interested anymore."

Teddy watched him sand beveled edges on the satinwood squares. On the stereo Mozart had reined himself in for an andante exactly the color of a November soul. "Do you still hang with the Seattle art crowd?" she asked.

"Actually, there are several crowds, none of which seems to remember my existence since I moved up here to become a paper-pushing drone. But I do try to get down for people's openings and stuff."

"Do you ever show yourself?"

"Me?" He looked surprised. "I'm not an artist."

Teddy gestured at the glowing woods. "But this stuff is really beautiful."

"This isn't *art*, this is craft. Jana's an artist, Eric's an artist. Artists have wings; I couldn't fly if my life depended on it."

A timer went off in the kitchen and Teddy hopped off her stool. "Well, I'd invite myself to eat your chicken but my sister'll be waiting to throw something in the microwave." She walked to the door and aimed a power smile. "I'll check back about the dictionary."

He smiled shyly and looked away. "No problem. I can have it for you tomorrow."

"Thank you. That'd be great."

"Well, good night."

"Good night." She slid the glass behind her and stood for a moment on his patio. Her silver breath rose buoyantly into the night.

5

Her front bell was ringing as Teddy slid closed the glass. Scurrying to the entry, she opened it to find Aurie Scholl holding fragrant bags of takeout food. He smiled through horn-rimmed glasses. "Hello."

"*Un*believable." She slammed the door.

The bell rang again and his muffled voice called through the panels. "Teddy, I was supposed to meet Tabor at a restaurant. She didn't show." In the hallway the aromatic bags had left their perfume. Opening the door slightly, she stared into his injured eyes. She moved back to let him in, then walked down the hall. "Where *is* Tabor?"

Aurie followed to the kitchen, pulling out styrofoam boxes and setting them on the counter. "As a matter of fact, she went to see a man about a cow."

"You really have a lot of nerve."

"Does that mean you're not even going to take my coat?"

She pointed toward the hall closet. "Out there."

Listening to him put away his jacket, she opened the refrigerator and splashed merlot into a glass, gulping down half. He walked into the kitchen, his nose, as usual, entering first. It was a fine nose, hooked and Gallic, but entirely out of its element in the yuppified Northwest. And he needed a haircut badly.

"Aurie, what are you *doing* here?"

"Aren't you going to offer me something to drink?"

"I don't keep designer beer."

"Water's fine."

She glared at his cautious face and noted with satisfaction that his sideburns were starting to gray. "Tap or mineral? Or Coke."

"Coke, please."

Teddy rooted for a can in the bottom of the fridge and topped off her wine glass for good measure.

His Coke can opened with a whoosh and he took a sip. "You look great."

"Thank you. You're looking older. More worn out."

Aurie combed his brown hair back with his fingers. "Tabor told me what happened last night. Want to talk about it?"

"With *you*?"

He sipped Coke again in the glacial silence. "Well, other than you've traumatized two-thirds of your frontal lobe, how's life?"

"Perfectly wonderful. No one's two-timed me in years." She flitted nervously around the room. "How about you? Still practicing extortion down there in Seattle?"

Eyes narrowed cautiously, he watched her dart around the kitchen. "Same O.R., same nurses, same knees. Only the names are changed to protect the innocent." Pushing his glasses up his nose, he switched gears. "Bought a house on Lake Washington. Just finished rebuilding the dock. I'm sort of rattling around in there by myself, though."

"Yes, I believe I heard about your marital problems."

He sipped Coke. "News travels fast."

"You should be proud of her. I hear she traded up."

"She did indeed." He nodded. "My only condolence is how cheap that made it for me. All I lost was the house and some cash. And her jewelry." He scowled. "People say when they start buying their own diamonds . . ." The sentence stumbled to a tragic death. "You're laughing."

Teddy stiffened her face. "No, I'm not." She swept into the living room and sat down on the couch. He followed, sitting opposite on the edge of the chair.

"Nice room." He gestured to the book-lined walls.

"Thank you." She glowered.

After a sip or two he tried again. "Tabor sure looks great. What a beautiful body."

Teddy blinked contemptuously.

"Although I halfway wondered if she wasn't on the juice."

"You mean steroids?"

"More like growth hormones these days. Her mandible doesn't exhibit any of the characteristic thickening, but the cuts on that woman are something else. Only ones I've seen deeper on a female were on a high-jumper I know was juicing it." He settled back into the cushions. "Want me to build a fire?"

"Oh, Aurie!" She leaped up, eyes crimson with rage. "You never change, do you?"

Long fingers pressing into the fragile aluminum can, he said ruefully, "I guess this means I don't ask you down to Seattle next weekend."

"Get out!"

"Teddy, I mean, can't we just talk? I just wanted to see you again."

"You've seen me, now go."

"You can't still be angry."

"Wrong! I will always be angry. And anytime in the future I am jilted for a woman with cuter kneecaps, I will be angry again."

"I never said she had cute knees."

"Liar!" She pelted. "The first thing you *ever* said about her was that the captain of the cheerleaders had patellas shaped like Happy Face."

"Yes, okay. I wanted to explain about that." He exhaled

and blurted his speech. "Obviously you don't understand what it's like to be world's biggest super-geek and have the captain of the cheerleaders smile at you."

"Aurie, that's so high school! How could you possibly buy into that?"

Fleetingly, his amber eyes remembered how easy it had been.

Crossing her arms, Teddy hovered like a gunship. "Aurie, it won't work. You're too self-centered, I'm too mad." She looked at the takeout cartons in the kitchen. "So please eat your dinner and go back to Seattle."

Stiffly he rose from the chair. "Shouldn't we wait for Tabor?"

"*We*? I'm not eating with you."

He stared blindly, then loped Aurie-like into the kitchen. Taking a deep breath, he molded his plastic face for his Robin Williams impersonation: "Where does the earthling keep her plates? I can't eat off styrofoam. It reminds me of a foo—"

"—a foot fungus. Above the dishwasher, Aurie."

"You know," he said cheerily, "I still use your mother's criterium of judging restaurants by the smell of the kitchen. This stuff is from the Lebanese restaurant on Samish." From the containers he scraped out barely cooked spinach with vinaigrette dressing, fragrant noodles that smelled of fresh-picked thyme, and delicate baby eggplants stuffed with pine nuts and garlic.

Hungrily from behind her wine glass Teddy watched him eat at the far end of the table. Occasionally Aurie tossed out a funny story about joint distress or ethnic food and watched it fall prostrate on the polished boards between them. Halfway through his meal he looked up and said, "This isn't very much fun, is it?"

"What did you expect?"

He finished in silence and picked up his dishes, carrying

them into the kitchen. Rolling up his sleeves, he opened the dishwasher.

"Just leave that," she said. "I'll get them."

"Nay, comely maid." He feigned heartiness. "Let it not be said that Aurelian Scholl sullies the domestic chastity of the," he turned a plate over and read, " 'Bakewell Oven-pruf, Milwaukee' without cleaning up his mess."

"Aurie, please don't do charming. If you knew how badly I wanted you out of my house right now, you wouldn't even try."

He pushed his glasses up his nose. "Then I guess I should go."

"You should."

There was a noise outside and Teddy rose to turn on the porch light. Seconds later Tabor burst in and dropped a white cylinder, an armload of books, and a decrepit fiberboard suitcase on the table. Looking back and forth between Aurie and Teddy, she gauged the temperature of the room. "Hope you guys are finished with formalities, I'm really hungry. Aurie, sorry I'm late, I called the restaurant and they said you left with takeout."

Teddy turned to the counter to fix Tabor a plate of food, which Aurie took as a signal to open the refrigerator. "Want a Coke, Tabor?" He pulled out another for himself.

"I don't do carbonation. Thanks, Teddy." She took her plate to the table and shoveled in a forkful of noodles. "It's been an *incredible* day." She patted the buckram suitcase beside her.

"What happened?" Opening his Coke, Aurie leaned against the counter.

Tabor chewed and swallowed, then stuffed in more noodles for security's sake. "Well, first of all, it turns out that March Hunt lives in a place so small, you have to patch in a telephone line through the Coast Guard short wave. No cell phone yet. They put you on this party line—the guardsman's kids are playing in the background, every boat on the west coast of Vancouver Island is listening in. Anyway, she was very spacey—Lieutenant Russell had to keep telling her everything three times.''

"What'd she say about Margaret?"

Tabor chased a piece of eggplant around with her fork. "At first she kept repeating things, like that's how she accepts bad news? I think she's old and lives alone.''

"Oh, dear.''

"Yeah, I know. And when we were just about to hang up, Russell asked if there was anything we could do for her and she said yes, there was: if Margaret still had their old doll valise, she'd really like to have it. She started describing it,'' Tabor gestured to the suitcase with her fork, ''and I knew exactly what she was talking about because it was right there on the shelf every time I walked into the barn.'' Not letting go of her fork, Tabor snapped open the rusty locks and let the lid fall back on the table. "Can you imagine asking for these?''

Inside were two decrepit Madame Alexander dolls lying in nests of aging doll clothes. *"Little Women.''* Teddy picked up one of the dollies. "I think this is Beth.''

Beth's crystal blue eyes were sunken in her head and the tip of her pert little nose was worn-away gray. Along her creamy forehead her black wig had peeled off and up close she smelled like the foxed pages of Nigel's antique books.

Aurie stepped forward. "Isn't *Little Women* your mother's favorite book?"

"Sorta,'' sniffed Tabor. "We're pretty sure it's the only thing she's read in English.''

"Wait a minute." Aurie narrowed his eyes. "I thought Marmee used to be a Shakespearean actress back in Italy.''

"Sorta.'' Tabor sniffed again. "We just tell people that. What she really did was stand on the balcony of the Castle Bella Guardia doing Juliet for English-speaking tourists.''

Teddy added, "The Verona Board of Tourism.''

Tabor gestured grandly. " ' 'Tis but thy name that is my

enemy. Thou art thyself, though, not a Montague.' "

Teddy laid down the capper: "Marmee says she never understood a word." In the silence she lifted the dolly skirt to peek at Beth's lacy knickers. "These dolls are really beautiful. Or at least, *used to be* really beautiful. Someone did a good job on the little clothes."

The dollies wore ruby velvet capes with shredded satin lining, and bombazine bonnets with balding rabbit trim. Each dolly had a pair of brittle patent slippers on her chunky feet; each carried a beaded opera purse the size of a dime.

Laying Beth next to her sister, Teddy said, "I can't believe Russell let you take all this. He wasn't even going to let you take *your* stuff last night."

Tabor got up and poured herself a glass of milk. "He checked them out first. He wasn't particularly interested in the barn. Your tires and my footprints were the only tracks back there."

"What'd you do with your cow?" asked Aurie.

"Boarded her down the road. They came and picked her up."

Teddy tucked the dollies into the suitcase and closed the locks. "What a touching thing to ask for. When is March coming down?"

"Never, as far as I can tell."

"Never?"

Tabor nodded. "All she said was she wants the body cremated and sent up when they're through with it. And anyway, I don't think she has transportation. So, very stupidly, I told her I'd bring the suitcase up there this weekend. Except she didn't tell me 'til after that I would have to rent a boat to get there."

"You're kidding? Where does she live?"

"Her mailing address is Gold River, that's got roads. But she lives in a place called Morgan Cove, out on the west coast of the island. Give me that map, I'll show you."

Teddy handed her sister the paper cylinder and Tabor unfurled a yellow and white nautical chart. The label announced it as Canadian Hydrographic Chart #3664.

Through the yellow land-mass of an unspecified portion of Vancouver Island, water intrusions spread like a Picasso-drawn woman with outstretched arms and a howling-dog head. Starting at the bottom left corner, her bell-shaped skirt was Nootka Sound billowing out into the wide Pacific. Nipped in at the waist between two points, she had a watery chest with yellow Bligh Island as ragged lungs. Out from the channels around Bligh, her two arms splayed off into the interior as snaking waterways. Up from her neck, her watery Cubist head jutted northeast in the form of Tlupana Inlet.

Tabor smoothed the chart and pointed to a spot on the waterwoman's wrist. "Here's Gold River. You follow this inlet down to Bligh Island. Morgan Cove is right on her shoulder, north of Bligh. March said if you put a boat in at Gold River you can be there in an hour."

"How far north is this? I can't tell."

"Halfway up Vancouver Island."

Tabor pointed to the waterwoman's chest. "Cook Channel. What do you think, Teddy: is that from Captain Cook?"

Teddy peered. "Oh, yes. He charted all this in the 1770s. And Bligh Island would have been for William Bligh. *Mutiny on the Bounty.*"

"What was he doing here?"

"Before the *Bounty*, he was the captain of the other boat with Cook. He was supposedly the best navigator in the world at the time. Actually, around here somewhere should be a place Cook made famous. Maybe it's not on this chart, though."

"Famous?" Tabor peered. "How come we've never heard of it?"

"It's a place called Friendly Cove. And for about thirty

years around 1800, it was one of the great trade centers of the world.'' Suddenly Teddy stabbed at a cove near the waterwoman's waist. ''There it is.''

Tabor squinted closely. ''What'd they trade?''

''Sea otter furs,'' said Teddy.

''For top hats,'' prompted Tabor.

''No, for the lining of Chinese winter robes. What happened was that when Captain Cook was up there charting, he acquired a single sea otter pelt and brought it to China where he found he could exchange it for the equivalent of, oh, five hundred dollars. He wrote about it in his journals, and by the late 1780s a wildly profitable trade triangle sprang up: Chinese tea to Europe, European manufactured goods to Nootka Sound, sea otter skins to China.''

''Gee, Teddy, too bad all the stuff you know is so useless.''

''Drop dead.''

Using her fingers for calipers, Tabor roughly measured the distance from Gold River to Morgan Cove. ''I've called Gold River and you can rent boats from a charter service, although they didn't sound enthusiastic when I told them it was just me. I had to lie and say I drive boats all the time.''

''Tabor!'' Teddy looked out at the silver drizzle. ''What's the weather like up there now?''

''Same as here.''

''Then I agree with the charter guys. I don't think you should go.''

''Not by myself.'' Tabor looked up expectantly. ''That's why I was going to ask you to come.''

''You're out of your mind! Tabor, you shouldn't be doing this to yourself, it's like sticking a finger in a wound. You need to leave it alone.''

''So you won't come with me?''

''Oh, Tabor. I can't anyway, I'm interviewing Walter Lloyd in the morning, and teaching in the afternoon. Why don't you mail her the dolls?''

With her fork Tabor pressed a lone pine nut into the tines. "March only picks up her mail every few weeks and it'll be a long time 'til she hits town again. Besides, I need to see her. I'm pretty sure she wants to tell me something about Margaret. She said she might have some information but doesn't know what to do with it."

"Tabor, please don't. You'll just get hurt."

Suddenly Aurie stepped forward. "Tabor, why don't I take you up? We can use my ski boat."

Tabor sprang from the chair. "Would you?"

"Provided I can get somebody to cover for me tomorrow. Let me make a few phone calls."

"Outstanding." Tabor pointed toward the phone on the end table. "You can take it to the kitchen."

"That's okay. Mine's in the car. I'll be right back."

Aurie went outside and they heard his car door slam. From the front porch he murmured into his cell phone, talking out into the rain. Teddy said, "Tabor, why'd you let him come?"

Tabor shrugged. "Free dinner."

"Thanks a lot for thinking about me."

"Aww, I knew you could handle him. You're little, but you're mean."

They waited, listening to Aurie make terse replies, signaling the end of his conversation. Moments later he came back into the room, beaming. "All set. All I have to do is cut off my right index finger when I get back."

"Excellent! What time?"

"I can be back up here by noon."

"Great." Tabor leaped up. "I'll make lunch. Do you like smoked tofu sandwiches?"

"Smoked!" Aurie slapped his face like Macaulay Culkin. "Tabor, that's my favorite way!" He loped to the closet and pulled out his jacket. "Well, it's been fun, Morellis. See you tomorrow."

"Bye, Aurie."

Teddy said nothing and he left.

"Jeez, he's a kick," said Tabor. "Did you guys work it out, about Jennifer and all?"

"We did not, and we're not going to, okay?" Crushing the empty styrofoam, she began eliminating all traces of Aurie.

"Hey! Don't do that. It lets fluorocarbons into the atmosphere." Tabor dashed over to husband the rest of the cartons into her own little corner of the counter. "Also, you've been putting all kinds of paper into your trash cans that ought to be recycled."

"Tabor, this is my house, I recycle what I want. And could you please get your barbell out of the living room? I don't want sweat all over the rug."

"Oh, that reminds me: a guy named Christian from down the row came by this morning: curly hair, seriously arrogant ass."

"Really?" Teddy lowered her eyes. "I hadn't noticed."

"Yeah, right," Tabor glanced at her sister's face. "Wow, look at you. Hey, isn't he kind of a baby-dude for you? I think he's a little young."

Teddy flushed, turning to the counter. "But look at the plus side: he's not an academic, his ego's under six figures—he doesn't even flirt."

"Pick up the clue phone, Teddy. Anybody looks like that already has a girlfriend. Or boyfriend, what-the-hey."

"No, he doesn't. Technically, he's got a wife, but she ran off. Right now he probably just needs someone to talk to."

"Which is, of course, the only thing you have in mind." Tabor watched her sister pad to the bookcase and pull down Eurich's *History of the Ancien Régime*. "What are you doing?"

"Christian seems a little tongue-tied. I'm going to try to bring him out."

"Yeah, I think I remember his telling me he's a French history buff."

"Not history, Dummo, French marquetry furniture of the eighteenth century. Then I'll move quickly on to wind resistance in windsurfing. I saw a *Scientific American* article about it in the dentist's office."

"God, you're weird."

"The French deconstructionists say that knowledge is very sexy."

"I sleep with my Britannica." Tabor raised a takeout carton to her mouth and shoveled in marinated spinach. "Know what else I did today?"

"Hey, wait a minute, Tabor. I haven't had anything to eat yet." Teddy marked the chapter on Louis XIV ébénists and attacked the noodle carton with a fork from the drawer. "Okay, what'd you do today?"

Tabor chewed spinach and gestured toward the thin volumes beside the valise. "I checked out some of Margaret's books from the library."

"What are they about?"

"Regular kids' stuff. They're not bad. *Yukon Boy* won an award, so I read that first. It's about a boy lost in the snow who sings with the wolves and they let him sleep in their den for the night."

She swallowed. "Then there's *Island Summer*. It's a tad slow. It's about an Indian girl on Vancouver Island who makes raspberry leaf tea and cooks clams on the beach."

"You've got three books."

"Last one's *Train to Ontario*. That's my favorite. It's about Margaret and March growing up, at least I think it is: two little girls and their mom take the Canadian Pacific across the Rockies in winter." She walked over and leafed through the book. "Listen to this and see if you can't imagine Margaret and March. 'Mary Beth examined the red braid on Annie's coat and realized the conductor had thought they were twins. Grabbing her sister's hand, she dragged her down the aisle to search for him. Finally she found him by the watercooler talking to the bald man from Goose River. Tugging on his stiff conductor's jacket, she said, "Annie's six. I'm seven. We look different under our coats." ' " Tabor looked up. "Isn't that sweet?"

"Positively saccharine."

"Actually, I was kinda hoping I'd find the clue about who murdered her, you know? Like somebody from the past?"

"No, Tabor, leave it to the police."

"A lot they care."

"Listen, Tabor, I didn't want to hurt your feelings before, but Lieutenant Russell is right, the kind of murder it is suggests that Margaret was dealing in drugs and what they stole were her computer records."

"Aarugh!" Tabor smashed Aurie's Coke can flat with her fist. "You're as bad as Russell."

"Okay, then: how *was* she supporting herself?"

"By eating oatmeal from the feed store and subletting to me. Teddy, she wrote *books*, whoever stole her disks wanted to eliminate something about her work. Get it?"

"Then let Russell take care of it."

"Are you kidding? I suppose you haven't lived here long enough to know what happens to homicides on Canadians. Anyway, those guys are total incompetents."

"No, they're not. What happens to Canadians?"

Tabor waved her fork. "The cases get caught up in jurisdictional disputes. Mounties don't like to work with cowboy Americans. The whole thing just drowns in a bureaucratic swill."

"Well I didn't think anybody seemed incompetent. Anyway, you thought Lieutenant Russell was doing a really good job this morning."

"I changed my mind. You should have seen him and these two other guys out at the farm. There's these extra tire tracks that run halfway up the drive, and these guys were like the Three Stooges, screaming at each other for letting so many cars run over them last night.

"And, then after, when I told them I had checked Margaret's books out of the library for clues, one of the guys goes, he goes like this—" Tabor rolled her eyes.

"That's because he knows more about murder investigations than you do."

"Not in this particular case."

"Well, Tabor, let me tell you something. I know I can't stop you from trying to help, but two things you're going to have to remember: if you get mixed up in this, you're going to be paying off lawyers 'til you die." Teddy tossed her fork into the sink. "And—if you get in *really* deep— Margaret's drug dealers are probably going to get you before the lawyers."

6

"Tabor! It's for you."

Blindly Tabor stumbled into Teddy's room and picked up the bedside phone. Neon digits glowed 2:08 a.m. "Hello?"

"Tabor?" It was Aurie. "I checked the map last night and this is harder than it looks. It's going to take us eight hours to get there."

"Eight hours!"

"The ferry leaves for Vancouver Island at 5 a.m. That means I pick you up in two hours. Are you packed?"

"Can't we take a later ferry?"

"Set your alarm. You can sleep in the car."

On the cardeck the ferryman waved them into a vaulted center lane so that their trailered boat would have plenty of headroom. Pulling up inches from the rig in front of them, Aurie set the hand brake and Tabor climbed out into the echoing tunnel. She stretched catlike in the chill air and looked back at their trailer for the first time, seeing that the boat they towed was not a Lake Washington pleasure craft; it was a welded aluminum, twenty-two-foot utility skiff with a boxy cabin and heavy duty hull.

"Aurie, this isn't a ski boat."

He zipped up his down vest. "After I left your house last night, I realized we were going to need something with a cabin on it. We don't want to be messing around on the saltwater in November.''

''Where'd you get this?''

''Charlie Tuna's.''

''You *rented* it?''

''I called him on the way home last night and met him at his yard. Charlie plays squash.''

Tabor bit her lip. ''Can I split the cost with you?''

''Nothing doing. My treat.''

''Thank you.''

They climbed the drafty stairs to the heated lounge and poured themselves hot drinks from the great stainless urns. Finding two facing benches in the corner, they nestled in the shadows as the ferry sang basso and rumbled away from the dock.

Tabor held up three fingers. ''Okay. One hour in the car, two on the ferry, then what?''

Aurie squinted past his reflection into the black morning. ''I figure four hours up to Gold River, then an hour out by boat. That should make it right after lunch, *if* we can find this woman in the first place.''

''You know, Aurie, I really appreciate your coming and everything. But if you think hanging out with me is going to win points with the Short Girl,'' Tabor shook her head, ''it just doesn't work that way.''

Aurie combed back his hair with his fingers. ''Tabor, you're looking at a desperate man here.''

''Oh, right.'' Tabor gulped herb tea and immediately went back to sleep. Aurie put his feet up and stared into the dark, watching Tabor sleep in the glass reflection. He tried to determine if the exquisite Morelli skin was perhaps one shade paler on Tabor, or identical to Teddy's. With a finger on the glass, he traced the outline of Teddy's cropped brown bangs as they framed her Hershey eyes. It was the Morelli health that made them so attractive, the capillary glow directly under the skin. He combed back his ragged locks with his fingers. She was right about his needing a haircut.

In the first light of morning they off-loaded at Nanaimo and followed the coastline up-island. They drove by sump- tuous retirement houses perched on bluffs, and cozy trailer courts left from the time when islands were still cheap. They passed sawmill cities with totem poles at the mall, and sweeping coastal bays as ravishing as memory.

After three hours of northing, they turned west and drove inland through the primeval forests of Strathcona Provincial Park. Climbing to high altitude, they hugged the shore of a pristine lake. From the cliffs, waterfalls dropped out of nowhere, spraying mist upon the asphalt. Down past the outfall of the lake, a boulder-strewn salmon stream sluiced over gravel bars and silver logs.

Finally they rolled from the hills down into the spectac- ular natural bowl circling the town of Gold River. Cliffs on three sides rose like brooding centurions, stalwartly bearing their powdery cloaks of early snow. On the fourth side the serrated hills receded in blue waves.

Pulling into a mini-mart for gas, Tabor leapt out. "I'll get it."

"Nonsense." The tank was on Aurie's side and Tabor deferred, leaning against the fender of his metallic brown Saab. "I'm surprised this has a trailer hitch."

"I had Charlie put one on last night."

"Aurie!"

He shrugged. "It needed one anyway." He went inside to pay, then called to an Indian attendant emptying trash cans. "Which way to the boat launch?"

The man stared, trying to figure out what Aurie was talk- ing about. "Oh. You mean down at the saltchuck." He waved south, down the valley. " 'Bout fifteen kilometers. End of the road."

Aurie climbed in and started the car. "Saltchuck?"

Tabor buckled her seatbelt. "Beats me."

Following the river down its tumbled valley, they came to a peculiar saltwater settlement: on one side of the road was a mammoth pulp mill spewing faux cumulus from its stacks, and on the other, a cozy Indian reserve of twenty houses humming like a day care center. In a graveled playground, raven-haired children hung from monkey bars and toddlers pushed their own strollers under the eyes of silver-haired grandmothers.

The road ended abruptly at the boat launch, a slimy concrete ramp disappearing into the jade-colored murk. At a wooden dock a small fishing fleet was tied up next to a portable aluminum building. Aurie backed the trailer down into the saltwater and Tabor climbed aboard, readying the lines. "Don't forget the dolls," she called as he went to park.

They cast off and motored out into Muchalat Inlet, a broad arm of sea twisting through the mountains of west Vancouver Island. Tabor inhaled the extravagant air and looked around. The morning was overcast and still. On both sides high sweeps of evergreen waited to become newsprint or two-by-fours, while back at the head of the inlet the pulp mill spewed stink with Surrealist shock tactics: the Industrial Revolution does Eden. Aurie throttled up and they sped through the hills out toward the big water.

Huddled in the little cabin, Tabor watched the chart as Aurie navigated down the channel, past anchored log booms and rotten pilings in coves. They ran due west for forty minutes, veering starboard around Gore Island. A few minutes later, Aurie throttled down as they rounded the point at Morgan Cove. They motored cautiously into the cove, not knowing what to expect.

"Oh, my!" gasped Tabor.

March Hunt's cove was a watercolor from a children's book. The tumbled hillsides were a hunting tapestry of lost secrets and tangled vines. Floating by a creek mouth was a whimsical two-room cottage on a spacious moveable raft.

The cottage wore flower boxes, an attic dormer, French blue trim. Through a bay window they could see shelves of market goods and a massive spinning wheel. Out on the raft itself were raised vegetable beds, two outbuildings, charming garden chairs, and a latrine. The place was a cross between Snow White's cottage and Mr. McGregor's garden.

Tabor squinted at a shingled sign. " 'Morgan Cove Store.' Boy, I hope she's got lunch stuff. I didn't get a chance to make sandwiches." She pulled out the suitcase, ready to disembark.

They puttered in and Aurie said, "I don't see a boat. I wonder if anybody's home."

Drifting up to the raft, they secured docking lines at the broad planked area used as a side yard. Tabor clutched the suitcase and hopped over dormant vegetable beds bounded by railroad ties. Shielding her eyes, she peeked through the bay window.

Directly in front of the window the outsized spinning wheel stood like a monument to female stamina, while along the far side of the room ran a glass storecase filled with expensive Haida silver and rare sea treasures. All around the room hung bright hanks of homespun wool and thick cheerful sweaters. Binoculars and sumptuous picture books were on the shelves, as were herbs, beans, boxed foods, and baking powder. Dangling next to the window was a collapsible plastic crab pot. The tag read "$52."

"No one's here," said Aurie.

"Darn it. She knew we were coming."

They walked around to the sturdy hand-wrought door. On the beveled glass was a hastily taped message: "Yu-quot."

"Yogurt," corrected Tabor.

"Tabor, this is the house of a perfectly literate woman. Yuquot's a place. We'll have to just leave the dolls. You can write her a note."

Tabor tightened her grip on the suitcase. "No."

Aurie gestured to the craggy mountains beyond the cove. "Tabor, we can't just run out there looking for her."

"Aurie, please. I've got to talk to her. One of the reasons I wanted to come is to check on her. She's taking Margaret's death really hard, I could tell on the phone. And I have to know if she's really got any ideas about who killed her sister."

"Tabor, listen to me." Aurie touched her forearms and made sincere eye contact. "I realize tracking down the killer is your way of dealing with grief, but in this case, you're playing with fire. How do you know you won't screw things up for the police?"

"Because they're not even trying, that's why."

"You don't know that."

"Yes I do. When I told Lieutenant Russell he needed to read her books, he looked at me like I stepped off of Planet Zircon. He has no idea what he's dealing with." Pressing the suitcase against the shingles with her hip, she zipped up her jacket. "Please, Aurie, can't we just wait a little while? She'll be back."

Aurie pulled a navy watch cap out of his pocket and stretched it over his unkempt hair. "Whatever we do, we need to get out of the wind."

Satisfied, Tabor turned up her coat collar. "I'm hungry." She gazed through the window at the vanilla wafers and canned hams for sale.

"I have M&Ms in the boat," Aurie said.

"I could do M&Ms." Tabor tucked the suitcase under her arm and headed for the skiff.

Standing in the close cabin, they shoveled candies into their mouths, crunching hungrily on the shells. Leaning against the console, Tabor studied the chart. "Where do you suppose Yuquot is? It couldn't be too far."

Aurie popped more M&Ms. "Doesn't matter if it's right

past the next stoplight, Dearie. If it's not on this chart, we can't go there.''

"Aha!" Tabor jabbed the chart and drooled red chocolate juice at the same time. Wiping off the chart, she added, "There. Right at the head of Nootka Sound." She pointed to a spot on the waterwoman's nipped waist. "How far is that, Aurie?"

"I don't know. Thirty minutes?" He scrutinized the tiny writing next to Yuquot. " 'F-Flashing 12 seconds.' There's a lighthouse."

"Hey! Yuquot is the name of the town on Friendly Cove. Isn't that the place Teddy said did fur trade?"

Aurie squinted at the markings. "This shows six buildings. If Friendly Cove used to be the center of the world, it's certainly gone downhill." He looked at his watch. "Well? It's two-thirty. Are we going?"

"Outstanding!" Tabor replaced the doll's suitcase under the console.

"You know," Aurie said. "There's a strong possibility we won't even find her. Why don't you leave the dolls in the shed, just in case? You can put a note on the door."

Reluctantly, Tabor gripped the suitcase handle. "I don't have any paper."

"Use the back of hers."

Tabor wrote a note and they cast off, huddled in the little pilot house. On both sides the rugged terrain had been relandscaped with extravagant plantations of Douglas fir in late stages of their sixty-year growth allotment. Occasionally they passed soul-rending clear-cuts, scathing reminders of what would happen to each hillside in turn.

They sped across the final reach to Friendly Cove, spying a spanking white lighthouse with red roof. Around its base was a cluster of workshops and houses, all red-roofed and freshly painted in government-issue white. Farther inland, behind a stand of trees, was a steepled little church of recent vintage and finally, in the heart of the cove, stood a totem pole and two large wooden houses. Down on the water were three docks: a foam-buoyed wharf for the lighthouse keepers, a high stationary pier for the weekly packet boat, and a low log-boom float in front of the Indian houses.

Scrutinizing the docks, Tabor said, "Nobody's at the packet boat pier. Would March visit the lighthouse keepers or the Indians?"

Aurie squinted. "Let's try the lighthouse. There's a very strange runabout tied at the end." He pulled up beside the boat and they gawked. The runabout was a homemade concoction of unpainted marine plywood drenched in a clear icing of resinous fiberglass. The wayward little pilot house was set with nine-paned cottage windows from salvage.

They made their way up the aluminum ramp, their footsteps echoing across the cove. They clambered up thirty dirt steps terraced by heavy timbers and as they neared the top a strange presence began to fill the air. Tabor looked up. From the crest of the hill a wild-haired woman stared down like a furied priestess. She had onyx eyes and steely tresses that swirled about like a squall. She wore a thick homemade sweater the color of vanishing islands, and a long gathered skirt over Vibram hiking boots. "Where's the valise?" she said.

Tabor smiled. "We left it inside your shed."

"Cretins!" she gasped. "Now we'll have to go home first. Come with me." Perplexingly, she sped uphill, gesturing to a woman in the kitchen window of the lighthouse residence. "The Huberts are lending us their equipment. If we hurry, we can get this over with today. Shouldn't take too long."

"Wait!" said Tabor. "A-Are you March Hunt?"

"Of course. What's your name?"

"I'm Tabor, and this is Aur—"

"Don't worry, Taper, there's plenty for everybody. I'll go halfsies with you." To make her point, she turned and faced them squarely, breathing foul air. "That's *half* for you two, *half* for me. That's my final offer.'' She dashed up the cliff into a shed.

Tabor and Aurie panted to the top, stopping at the door of the dark shed. Inside March hovered over two sets of scuba gear: tanks, vests, wetsuits, duffels stuffed with fins and masks. ''Good thing you brought the man. You!'' she barked at Aurie, ''take this tank and duffel.'' Sizing up Tabor, she said, ''Girlie, you get these other two. I can handle the rest. And if Mrs. Hubert comes out,'' she lowered her voice to a hiss, ''don't breathe a word; the old cow thinks we're going after my fish trap. I told her I lost it in the cove.''

''March!'' Tabor grabbed both sides of the door frame. ''What's the matter?''

''I was a friend of your sister's, I lived at her house. I'm really sorry she died.''

''Yes, of course, we'll talk tonight. The important thing is to get on with the job before we lose more daylight.'' March leaned over and gathered scuba gear.

''Wait, March, we don't know what you're talking about. I brought the dolls. Don't you want them?''

March started suddenly. ''She didn't tell you?''

''Tell us what?''

''Oh, my. This changes everything.'' Biting her lower lip, she dragged Aurie's tank to the door, then gave up. ''You, come get this.'' Waving again to Mrs. Hubert in the window, she mouthed a grin. ''Stupid as a lima bean.''

Tabor stared at March's handknit sweater, thick as sheepskin, matted like felt. ''March, will you tell us what this is all about?''

''Of course. I have to.'' She picked up a duffel. ''I'm far too old to do this myself. Come on, we need to move fast if we're going to finish today.''

They carried the scuba gear down the slippery grade to the wharf. Dropping her duffel beside their boat, March untied her own docking lines. ''Put the gear in *your* boat, it's sturdier." Nose to nose with Aurie, she shouted, "D'you skipper?"

"Yes."

"We're taking the inside route to Morgan Cove. Follow *directly* behind me or you'll hit the shoals."

"Yes, ma'am."

Climbing into her dilapidated runabout, March drove briskly across the open stretch of Nootka Sound then suddenly veered to port at Bligh Island. Whisking past craggy bluffs, she led them so close to jagged shore they could see colonies of orange starfish and the wave-washed beards of purple mussels. Steering between sandstone islets, she zipped around a rocky point where a colony of surprised seals were sunning themselves on an invisible reef six inches under the water. As the boats approached, the shimmering herd undulated in a single torpid wave, disappearing into the sea.

"God, Aurie, this is dangerous."

He said nothing, then finally blurted, "I can't talk now. I have to concentrate."

March led them past ragged volcanic boulders that told a violent past and creamy cliffs stained with the blood of ferric elements. Finally rounding the point at Morgan Cove, she suddenly geared down and Aurie followed, letting out a deep sigh. They tied up at March's side yard as the old woman was already bringing the valise back from the shed. Clanging like a cuckoo clock, she said, "Come in. Come in."

They followed her into the store and watched openmouthed as she crossed the room, opening the valise and dumping the dolls on the floor. Striding back to the kitchen, she set the valise on the table and took out a carving knife, ripping the upper lining with a jerk. "Bah!" she said in disgust.

"March, stop!" cried Tabor.

Next March slashed the bottom of the case, suddenly

dropping the knife and plunging her hand into the blanched satin lining. "It's here! It's here!" She pulled out a faded yellow document and danced like a maniacal gnome. Tabor and Aurie watched dumbfounded as she unfolded the paper and flattened it out on the table, murmuring happy conversation under her breath.

Tabor peered. The creamy paper was a primitive map drawn in black ink. All that was shown was a tortured north-south shoreline peaking in a snoutlike point labeled "Boston." The chart had no scale: it could have been the American East Coast, it could have been right outside the door.

Stabbing at a circled X inside a shoe-shaped cove, March cackled like a crow. "Santa Gertrudis Cove, of course! Why didn't I think of that?" She turned to Tabor. "Not Boston Point. You can't drive a ship onto a point, can you, Girlie? You drive your ship into a cove."

"What it this?" asked Tabor.

March cocked her head like a pirate. "A treasure map, matey. Eh, eh, eh."

"Wait a minute." Aurie examined the laid out map. "You want *us* to dive to a shipwreck?"

"Thou Beamish Boy." She taunted him with Lewis Carroll.

Tabor leaned over. "What's there?"

March sneered. "What's there, what's there." She darted outside and disappeared into a shed, returning with a pair of fishermen's waders and a long-handled metal detector. Sitting at the table, she unlaced her hiking boots. "You two *do* you know how to dive, don't you? Any fool could do it with the vests nowadays."

"March," Aurie said. "You've got to slow down."

"No, Beamish. You're wrong. I'm fifty-nine years old, I don't have time to slow down."

Aurie blocked out the map with his large hand. "It's too dangerous. You don't know what you're doing."

March pointed to the inky X. "Four fathoms. You could do that holding your breath."

"March, listen to me. Last summer I had the privilege of diving at Port Royal in the Caribbean and the first thing I learned about shipwrecks is that you have to do your research topside—before you go down. It makes it much easier to work underwater. For instance, do you know what kind of ballast they used on this ship?"

"Ballast? I'm not interested in ballast!"

"Well, you should be. Anybody going after a shipwreck needs to know what's scattered on the bottom: river rock, Liverpool brick, olive oil jars. You find the right kind of ballast, you're guaranteed to find everything else close by."

"No, Beamish, you don't understand." Hands trembling, March pointed to a cluster of fat freckles in the center of Santa Gertrudis Cove. "See these rocks? I *know* these rocks. I know the bird shit on top of them, the mussels in the cleft there. This map is as detailed as knitting instructions. And as for what's there, that's my private business."

"Really? Are you certain of your amount? How do you know it's actually worth your while?"

March eyed him keenly. "You've come to steal my treasure, haven't you, Beamish?"

Aurie took off his glasses and rubbed his eyes. "March, you may not believe this, but I'm not actually interested in your treasure. If there's any diving to be done, I just want to make sure it's done safely, and legally as well."

Tabor crossed her arms. "Well, I think you're demented. And I'm not diving."

"Oh, *you* again." March glanced out the window to measure the light. "Meanwhile the chariot of the day *races* across the sky." She sat up straight, looking at Tabor as if for the first time. "Very well," she appraised her dull-witted pupil. "If I can convince you that the treasure belongs to me—me and *Margaret*, of course—will you dive?"

"No." Tabor reached down and swooped the dollies off the floor, sitting them on the table like little witnesses. "I came up here to help you through Margaret's death, and this is making me angry, and confused, and, I don't know. I'd just rather go home. Aurie?"

March leaped up. "No, you can't go. I haven't told you who killed Margaret yet."

"You don't know."

"Yes I do. I do. And I'll be glad to tell you if you help me with this wreck."

"Why haven't you called the police yet?"

"Well, you see, it's like I have *information* about who killed her, but I don't know what I have. Understand? And when you called yesterday and said Margaret'd been killed, I began thinking about . . . who to give it to."

"Give it to *me*."

"Well, I will." March batted her eyes coyly. "But like I said, only in fair trade: you dive, I deal."

Tabor stood rigid by the table. "How do I know this is the real thing?"

"It is, Girlie. No doubt about that." March pulled off her Vibram boots. "Now, who's going to wear the big scuba suit? It doesn't look like either of you can fit in Hubert's little one, does it?"

7

Teddy woke up that morning to find both Tabor and all the instant oatmeal gone. Microwaving what was left of the Lebanese dinner, she dressed and went out into the satin drizzle. The morning was as soft as eiderdown, the air thick as clotted cream. Out on the empty lakeside road the luminous pavement shone pearly gray in the filtered light and once again she envied the windsurfers—or anybody, for that matter—who could play hooky at eight-thirty Friday morning.

Arriving at Lloyd's estate, she steered slowly through the rhododendron thicket, trying to imagine what springtime was like when the grove was solid red flowers. She rounded the crest of the last hill, and started suddenly, "Oh, dear," veering off the road. A white sheriff's car was parked by Lloyd's back door.

Pulling up beside the vehicle, she looked in the kitchen window to see Mrs. Dykstra talking to two officers. The nurse motioned through the glass for Teddy to use the back steps, then came over to open the door.

Teddy clutched her book satchel and entered the kitchen, smiling feebly at the two deputies who leaned against the counter. One was handsomely Hispanic and tall. His name-tag said Martinez. The other was of medium height with more belly than was officially approved of. His name was

Dawson. Neither had questioned her the other night.

"Good morning," she said brightly. "Did you find the killer?"

Martinez turned down the squawk on his portable. "What? Oh, we're just waiting for the ambulance."

"Ambulance?"

The deputies looked at Mrs. Dykstra who then leveled her eyes at Teddy. "I'm afraid we have some very bad news." She arched her brow to take aim. "Mr. Lloyd had another stroke last night. He's dead."

"No!" Teddy looked back and forth among the three of them. "But he seemed so happy yesterday. Oh, I hope I didn't make him strain himself. I'm *so* sorry."

Satisfied, Mrs. Dykstra turned to the deputies. "She and Mr. Lloyd talked for most of the afternoon. We'd been having problems with his blood pressure and I'm afraid that might have been just enough to put him over the top."

Teddy bit her lip. "I'm *so* sorry."

Avoiding Teddy's eyes, Mrs. Dykstra glanced at her watch. "Maybe you'd better tell the deputies what you did for so long yesterday. It might help them fill out their report."

"All we did was talk! He was so happy doing it, I just let him go."

Dawson clattered his clipboard on the table. "Actually, I think we have all we need right here. Even if he did get worked up, it looks like a pretty straightforward seizure."

Mrs. Dykstra thrust her hands into her smock pockets. "A stroke is not a seizure, officer. A stroke is a cerebro-vascular accident."

Dawson scribbled on his clipboard. "Yes, ma'am, CVA. We got that." Tucking his pen in his pocket, he smiled soberly at Teddy. "It doesn't look like you'll be doing much interviewing today."

"I guess not." She looked at Mrs. Dykstra to see if there was any more blame to be laid. "Well, it won't do me any good to hang—wait! He has my tape recorder. May I go get it?''

The nurse shrugged and Dawson took command. "Sure. Officer Martinez can take you up."

The tall officer escorted Teddy through the long front room and up the open staircase. "Quite a place, isn't it?"

"Mr. Lloyd said they modeled it after Mount Hood Lodge."

"Hate to get termites."

They approached the bedroom, becoming silent. Officer Martinez reached for the doorknob. "This isn't going to spook you, is it?"

"I hope not. We'll see."

Mr. Lloyd lay in the middle of the bed, head centered on the pillow, a clean sheet pulled up to his chin. Teddy tiptoed across and unplugged her tape recorder from the bedside outlet. Winding the cord between elbow and hand, she silently said a prayer for the late Walter MacFarlane Lloyd.

Up close he was waxen. He lay with eyes closed, chin to the ceiling, his lower lip bitten through by his bottom teeth, as if he had fought death every inch of the way. Picking up her equipment, Teddy nodded to Officer Martinez, who led her out. They closed the door behind them and exhaled loudly.

"I wish he hadn't died."

Officer Martinez smiled sympathetically.

Down in the kitchen, they found Mrs. Dykstra on the phone and Dawson talking in low tones to Christian Wells, Lloyd's office manager, who had just arrived in a black Jeep Cherokee. Not wanting to disturb Mrs. Dykstra on the phone, Christian greeted Teddy with only a sober smile. In return, Teddy raised her eyebrows.

Padding over to her side of the room, Christian whispered, "If I had remembered you were coming today, I would have called and saved you the trip." The deputies tiptoed into the dining room to commune with the squawk on their portables.

Teddy asked, "Then you've already been here this morning?"

"Oh, yeah. Mrs. D. called me at six-thirty. She thinks he died sometime around midnight." He turned to watch Mrs. Dykstra hang up the phone. "Was that his daughter?"

"It was her housekeeper again. Angela's still in Palm Springs and they can't get in touch. Do you need her number?"

Christian glided over to the coffeemaker and poured himself a cup. "I'm sure we have it at the office someplace. Coffee anybody?" He was asking Teddy.

"No, thank you."

He sipped coffee and said, "Mrs. D., I *do* need to go through Mr. Lloyd's desk. He kept some files here and the lawyer wants everything."

Officer Dawson stamped into the kitchen. "Here they come!"

A white ambulance emerged from the trees and the deputies shuffled outside to wait.

Teddy stirred. "Well, I guess I'd better be going." To pack her things, she set the recorder on the table and popped Lloyd's second tape from the tape deck. Turning to Mrs. Dykstra, she held up both cassettes. "You might tell Mr. Lloyd's daughter that he made four of these for the Western Archives. I don't think she'd be interested in the verbal stuff, but he said he was going to sing missionary hymns last night, and if he did . . ."

Mrs. Dykstra glanced from the corner of her eye. "Oh, don't worry about that. He was singing up a storm last night. As a matter of fact, I wouldn't be surprised if you don't have it recorded right there the exact moment he died."

Teddy held the tapes at arm's length. "Oh, yuck."

Dykstra shrugged. "Maybe not. Maybe Mr. Lloyd had turned it off by then."

Outside paramedics unloaded a gurney from the back of the van and sprang the legs up to full height. With burdened arms Teddy walked to the door; Christian paced forward to open it.

"Thank you," she said.

"I feel terrible about your tapes. You want me to listen to them first, just in case?"

She stepped back, his muscled presence too intense. "No thank you. But that's a nice offer. I need to listen to it all anyway. I'll just try to steel myself." She turned. "Goodbye, Mrs. Dykstra. Thank you for everything."

The nurse looked out the window.

Driving silently back to campus, Teddy parked the car and walked over to Media Services, waiting at the counter while the student attendant made high-speed copies of the tapes. She chatted aggressively, thankful that the student hadn't the faintest notion she had just worked a man to death and was now flirting shamelessly with his office manager.

Sneaking up to her office, she closeted herself in and stared out the window. A minute later there were three smart raps on the door.

"Come in, Nigel."

He slipped in and leaned against a file cabinet, reeking naphtha. "I waited for your call the entire evening."

"Oh, Nigel, I'm sorry. I completely forgot."

"You could have at least had the courtesy to call back and say you weren't interested."

She exhaled, like a dolphin coming up for air. "Nigel." She held up the tapes. "The man I interviewed yesterday just died of a stroke—I might even have it recorded on tape. Not only that, his nurse is saying I'm the one who killed him because I got him so excited."

Nigel's mouth opened in sympathy. "Dear girl. The woman should be hung by her thumbs. You know you didn't have a thing to do with it, don't you?"

"No. Actually I don't. I know Mr. Lloyd would have died sometime. But I have no idea if it would have been next week or five years from now. Do you?"

Nigel shrugged. "Did he lead a fruitful life? Did he accomplish all he wanted to accomplish? If I were you, I wouldn't worry about it." He gazed on her piteously. "Poor you. All this after that murder the other night. Can I do anything?"

"I don't think so. Actually, I'd like to be alone, if you don't mind. I need to make a directory for the tapes while they're still fresh."

"What are you going to do if you come to his dying?"

She shrugged. "Listen. What am I supposed to do?"

"Don't play them yet, I can come over tonight."

She stiffened. "No, that's okay, I've got to do it anyway."

"Call me if you need anything." He patted her awkwardly on the shoulder and left the room.

Teddy slipped tape number one into the machine and turned it on. She listened with dread as it hissed a few loops of static, then popped alive with a rustle of papers.

"This is Walter MacFarlane Lloyd. It is nine o'clock on Thursday, November sixth. I am at my family home, *Saghalie Illahee*, and I am recording Chinook hymns for Dr. . . ." He had forgotten her name. "Dr. Teodora Morelli of the Rainwater University history department. This first song was one used by Methodist missionaries at the reservation, it's called 'Whiskey.' I learned it from Jesse's mother who sang it when she ironed. I'm looking at the first verse which literally translates, 'Formerly I loved whiskey, Formerly I loved whiskey. But now I *throw it away*.' Are you ready?" In a huffy baritone, Lloyd began.

"Ahnkuttie nika tikegh whiskey
Ahnkuttie nika tikegh whiskey
Pe alta nika mash."

He sang all four verses, each of which told of the ills of drinking and ended with the line "But now I throw it away." And through the tape Teddy could hear him heartily "throw it away" when he came to "*Pe alta nika mash.*"

Barely stopping for breath, Lloyd turned a leaf and said, "Okay, this next song is called 'Sunday' and you sing it to the tune of 'Come to Jesus.' Basically each of the four verses repeat the rules of Sunday three times. They are: 'Come to church, come to church, come to church. Today, today. Don't work, don't work, don't work. Today, today.' Then we have the same thing with 'Don't buy—today,' and 'Get the God talk—today.' The double line at the end of each verse, '*okoke sun*' means 'this sun,' or 'today.' "

"Chako yakwa, chako yakwa, chako yakwa
Okoke sun, okoke sun."

Teddy listened anxiously as Lloyd sang through the verses, knowing that at any moment might he might break into dire gasps. She punched off the machine, unable to bear the irony of his enthusiastic singing. She spent the rest of the morning staring out the window.

At lunchtime she came out to swallow two bites of pizza, and in the afternoon taught her seminar on automatic pilot. At five o'clock she drove home in the early twilight and collapsed on the couch. Book satchel on her lap, she lay in the dark, watching the yellow lights blink on around the lake: families arriving home to begin the dinner hour, all blissfully unaware of the random pain that could be dumped on their heads at any given moment. Time passed and she thought of nothing. Suddenly, a black shadow on the patio stepped out from behind the woodpile. She sucked in breath, motionless.

Raising its arm, the specter rapped on the glass. Teddy exhaled. It was Christian. He was wearing a black wetsuit and booties, and under his arm he carried a manila folder.

She slid open the door. "Interesting attire for Friday night, Mr. Wells."

He smiled beautifully. "I was going windsurfing and I thought I'd drop off the Chinook dictionary. May I come in?"

She stepped back and switched on a lamp. "Isn't it a little dark for windsurfing?"

"Actually, I like it this way. I can see them, they can't see me. Anyway, after work is the only time I have in winter, gets dark so early." He was standing close, wetsuit sculpting the elegant curve of his shoulders and the long muscles of his thighs. Handing her the folder, he said, "I tried not to handle it much. It's really brittle."

She opened the folder. "Ugh. You're right. I should take it up to Rare Books and let them make me a working copy. Then I can return this to you."

"How are your tapes coming?"

"Slowly. It's so painful to listen to him, I can barely do it. I'll have to knuckle down this weekend." She pulled the tapes from her satchel and tucked the dictionary in. Casually she said, "Want to hit a late movie tonight?"

Christian took a step backward. "Uh, I need to sand some maple."

"Sure." She mumbled, "And I ought to work on my tapes."

"Oh, I forgot: I talked to Lloyd's daughter today and told her about your tapes. She's really pleas—" The phone rang and he stopped. "Go ahead."

Teddy picked up the receiver.

"Short Girl?" It was Tabor. "I'm on Aurie's cellular." She went silent. ". . . hear me?"

"Just a minute, Tabor. Let me try loudspeaker."

"Hello, Shorts?" Tabor filled the room.

"Hi. Did you find March?"

"Not only did we find her, we're now helping her with one of the biggest underwater coups on the West Coast, ever. Aurie says people can eavesdrop on cellulars, so I can't exactly tell you what I'm talking about, but all I can say is that we're on to something really big and we really need your help."

"What for?"

"Okay. Tomorrow morning we need you to bring up eight tanks of scuba oxygen and a pair of mens' large waterproof booties—Aurie's leak."

"You're diving for a shipwreck?"

Across the room Christian cocked his head.

"Teddy, quiet. Aurie said not to say anything. Anyway, here's the poop: you want to make the 5 a.m. ferry out of Tsawwassen, which means you have to go the dive store tonight, so hurry, because it closes at nine. Also, get a pencil and I'll give you Aurie's Visa number to pay for everything."

"Tabor . . ."

"It takes a long time to get here, so you really don't want to miss the ferry."

"Tabor, I'm not coming."

"But you have to! The second set of scuba gear is a women's small, so Aurie's diving by himself. It's highly dangerous."

"I don't care if he's diving with mermaids. I can't come. Remember the guy I interviewed who speaks Chinook? Well, he just died on me."

"Bummer. Gee, Teddy, I'm really sorry. But you've still got to come. If we do this for March she said she'll tell us something about who killed Margaret. Please? You're much better at figuring things out."

"Tabor, listen to me: I can't."

Tabor's disappointment flooded the room. "Well, good-*bye*. Okay?" She hung up.

Christian was wide-eyed. "What was that all about?"

Teddy shook her head. "Tabor went up to deliver some dolls on Vancouver Island. I have no idea why they're scuba diving."

"It sounds like they're on to some really big shipwreck." Christian fidgeted with excitement.

"You don't understand. Everything Tabor does is really big."

"And she said somebody would tell her who killed Margaret Zimmerman, didn't she? You need to go help her."

"Wrong. She needs to leave it alone and I need to stay here and do my work."

Christian adjusted his rubber suit. "That's too bad. It sounds like they've got something going. Where is she exactly?"

"A place called Morgan Cove. It's barely on the map."

The phone rang again. Teddy answered. "Hello?"

"Teddy, listen to me."

Teddy rolled her eyes for Christian and punched loudspeaker again.

"Teddy, March Hunt knows Chinook. She said she'll write down a whole bunch for you if you come up here with the stuff."

"She does?"

"Yeah, like saltchuck means saltwater."

"I know that already. What else?"

Crossing the floor, Christian touched Teddy on the shoulder. "May I talk to her?"

Unzipping his insulated collar, Christian trembled in front of the phone. "Hello, Tabor? This is Christian Wells, I'm the one who came by yesterday. It sounds like you've found something important."

"Really important."

"Wooden or metal?"

"Well, the part you mean is wooden. But Aurie found exactly what we're looking for and it's metal. He says it's just sitting on the bottom in twenty feet of water."

"You're kidding." Christian twitched. "And you don't want to tell us what or where?"

"Aurie says not to. Ask Teddy where, she knows."

"Listen, I've done quite a bit of cold water diving and I'd be glad to help you out. Is there really somebody diving alone?"

"Yeah. And he's a moron."

"I can come tomorrow morning. What did you say I should bring?" Christian grabbed a pencil.

"Eight air tanks and a pair of men's large booties. Also, we need two heavy-duty airbags or floatbags, Aurie didn't know what they'd be called."

"Airbags."

"You don't have any, do you?"

"No." Christian's face clouded. "And I think they have to be special ordered at the dive shop."

"That's okay. Aurie says we might be able to get them in Vancouver. Also, you'll have to rent a boat to get here, so let me give you Aurie's Visa number to pay for everything."

"I have a boat. What else?"

"Sleeping bag, warm clothes, usual stuff."

"Pretty remote, huh?"

"Pretty cold, too."

"And Teddy can tell me how to get there?" He looked at her expectantly.

Teddy shrugged. "Sure, I'll show you."

"Thank you!" he beamed.

Tabor yelped delightedly. "Outstanding! You guys are great. See you tomorrow."

Flushed, Christian hung up the phone.

"Christian," said Teddy. "You can't leave town with the funeral coming up."

His green eyes danced. "Are you kidding? This is a perfect way to lay low. The lawyer thinks I'm going to do all his paperwork for him. And besides, we can't move on anything until Angela gets here."

"Why in the world are they diving for a shipwreck? Tabor went up to deliver some dolls."

Sweat beaded on Christian's upper lip and under the slick rubber his deltoids bulged like saltwater taffy. "Guess we'll find out when we get there."

"We?" Teddy eyed the elegant sweep of his cheekbones. "Christian, *I'm* not going."

"But you said you'd show me . . ."

"I meant I'd show you on the map."

His face dropped. "I thought . . . boy, did I blow that. Well, I don't want to go if you're not going."

Teddy's heart beat a scrambled tattoo. "Really?"

"I'm sorry. I thought you meant you might like to . . ."

"I would. I mean," she looked at him, searching. "I guess I could go. If March Hunt knows Chinook, it certainly wouldn't be a wasted trip." She touched the cassettes on the table. "And I can make a tape directory when I get back."

Christian wiped sweat off his forehead and further unzipped his wetsuit, this time to his waist. "This is great!" he said. "Aren't you excited?"

Teddy shrugged, patently ignoring his sculpted abs.

Christian padded to the glass door and turned. "I'll call you when I get back from the dive shop. I've got to get out of this wetsuit right now, it's too hot."

She poked her hands in her pockets. "Sounds like a good idea to me."

8

Around ten the next morning Teddy stretched extravagantly in the plush leather seat of Christian's Cherokee. Outside was the enormous sweep of Oyster Bay, Vancouver Island. "How long have we been traveling?" she asked. She glanced sideways and noted that his forest-green turtleneck picked up the plaid of his Black Watch shirt. Her heart raced at the thought of a man who could match his own clothes.

Christian punched a button on the jetlike console. "Six hours, fourteen minutes. We're averaging forty-nine miles per hour and consuming." He punched again. "16.8 miles per gallon. Anything else you want to know? Wind speed? Ambient temperature?"

Teddy grinned. "How long have you been doing marquetry?"

Christian turned a knob incrementally, asking for air warmed to seventy-one degrees. "Couple years. Ever since I realized I couldn't draw."

"You shouldn't be so hard on yourself. It really is a great skill. Some of the French ébénists in the eighteenth century just knock my socks off."

He looked over brightly. "You mean André-Charles Boulle and all them?"

"Yeah. All those swooping curves and tortoise shell

scrollwork they did for Louis XIV, that's really great stuff.''

"Too fancy. I prefer the Dutch. More respect for materials.''

Teddy turned. "I disagree. An old boyfriend of mine inherited a little Boulle writing table. I thought the scrollwork was perfectly appropriate for the design.''

Christian punched a button that told him he was headed west-northwest and now getting 15.3 miles per gallon. "With all due respect to your former boyfriend, what he probably has is a nineteenth-century piece *in the manner* of Boulle. There are only two documented pieces attributed to Boulle directly.''

"Really?" Teddy squirmed in her seat.

"Yeah. Boulle's atelier burned down in 1720 and the inventory loss was staggering. Not only furniture, but also a Correggio from his personal collection, a Raphael, and a sketchbook of Rubens.''

"I didn't know that. Guess what? The same former boyfriend is the man diving up at Morgan Cove with Tabor. Maybe you can tell him his writing table is a fake.''

"Ha! Just what I need: a punch in the face." The cellular phone rang and Christian picked up the receiver. "Yo?"

Teddy turned discreetly to the saltwater view, as if averting her eyes would also avert her ears.

Listening to a monologue from the other end, Christian twitched like a man with a sour stomach. Finally he asked, "Does he know the driver has since died?" He listened again, all the way through the coastal town of Campbell River and into the dark cathedral of old growth fir. "You were the one who said file an appeal!" Patiently he listened, swerving dangerously on a curve. "Listen," he said. "I can't talk right now. I'll have to call you back." He hung up, and there was an awkward silence.

Cheerily Teddy said, "You're having legal problems.''

Christian arched his back. "Nothing we can't work out.

There's some new people at the EPA and we're still learning how to dance together.''

Teddy ventured: ''Environmental Protection Agency.''

''That's right. They monitor our toxic waste.''

''Was your driver doing something illegal?''

''Technically he wasn't *our* driver. We had this old guy, Jesse, who drove truck for Mr. Lloyd. When he retired we set him up as an independent hauler to carry waste. As it turned out, instead of trucking our pentachlorophenol down to Arlington, Oregon—where it belonged—he was taking it up in the hills and dumping it. Now he's dead and the EPA is screaming bloody murder.''

''Jesse was the one Mr. Lloyd spoke Chinook with.''

Christian glanced over appreciatively. ''That's right. You two must have really gotten into it the other day.''

''We did.''

Christian's brow furrowed as he watched the road. ''It really laid him flat when Jesse died last year. Especially the way they found him. In retrospect, that was the beginning of the end for Mr. Lloyd.''

''What happened?''

''Jesse had gone into the wood kiln to keep warm and drink, and he passed out. They found him three days later behind a unit of Doug fir. He was tanned like leather, about half his regular body weight.''

''Yuck.''

''Yeah, the guy on the forklift hurled his breakfast.''

Teddy's eyebrows formed a troubled line. ''But Mr. Lloyd said Jesse had given up drinking.''

''Yeah, we were all trying to keep it from him so he wouldn't have to fire Jesse again. He had already done it twice in the past and it just about killed him both times. Makes me wonder if anybody *ever* gets to run a business based totally on management principles.'' Suddenly Christian jammed on the brakes. ''Will you look at that!''

A young buck with a stubby rack stood in the road

calmly observing their approach. His russet cloak glowed like a monarch's velvet; his shimmering rack was the color of wet peat. Turning his head with the bored gaze of the idle rich, he sauntered off into the salmonberries, disappearing without a trace.

"God, they're getting uppity." Christian glanced back in the rearview mirror. "I should have brought my bow."

"A Bambi killer, huh?"

"Bambi, Dumbo. The whole crowd." He glanced sideways to savor her distress. "My dad's from Montana. We always had at least one dead Bambi in the freezer each winter."

"Did you grow up there?"

"No, Yakima. How about you?"

"Seattle. My dad designed cockpits for Boeing."

"Really? Your sister talked like you guys were hardcore Italian. Capital Hill, Holy Names, mucho siblings . . ."

"I've always thought of it as hardcore Seattle."

"What's your sister's name again?"

"Tabor. She named herself that from a little drum she got for Christmas when she was six. She hates Tomasina."

"Wow. I don't blame her. Are the rest of you guys named like that?'

"Delizia, Elisabetta, Teodora, Tomasina, Raffaele, Carlo. Only my oldest brother got away clean—he's Joseph Morelli, Junior."

"So your dad's American?"

"We're all American. Dad's family has been in Seattle since the 1890s. Mom's the one born in Italy."

"How'd they meet?"

"Dad was with a Boeing trade delegation trying to sell jets to Air Italia, and my mother's acting group did some Shakespeare at a party the airline threw."

"Must have been selling 707's back then."

"I don't think my dad could have told you. All we heard is that Mom wore this little Juliet cap and laced-up costume, and Dad couldn't take his eyes off her.''

"Ha! Old people crack me up. Your dad retired?''

"He died four years ago. Heart attack.''

"Sorry. That's rough.''

"How about you? You mentioned a little brother, how old's he?''

"Eric? Twenty-four.''

"And you must be, what,'' she glanced over, "twenty-nine?''

"Twenty-eight.''

"Oh.''

They drove through the town of Gold River and followed the tumbling stream down to where it finally quieted at the saltwater. Ignoring the outrageous pulp mill on the right, they glanced across the road to the cozy settlement where Saturday morning flickered on TV sets behind picture windows.

They parked next to a portable aluminum office that advertised rental seaplanes and boats, and Christian climbed out. "I want to look at the boat ramp before we try it.''

"Good plan.''

They ambled over to the ramp to find three black-eyed boys in on-line skates skimming down the slope and turning at the last second before they hit the icy water. From the looks of their pants, they hadn't always been successful.

The boys stopped playing.

"Do you know March Hunt?'' asked Teddy.

Their patent-leather eyes stared as if she were deranged.

"She runs a store at Morgan Cove,'' Teddy coached.

"Oh, her.'' The skaters muscled their way uphill.

"How long does it take to get there?''

The boys went silent, never in their lives having considered anything so ridiculous as timing a trip on water. Without answering, they skated off toward Saturday morning, looking back occasionally to make sure the tourists hadn't fallen in, or hurt themselves.

Teddy looked down the slimy concrete slope. "Christian, guess what? Tabor has the nautical chart and I have no idea how to get to Morgan Cove without it."

"You're kidding." He spun around to look at the paper mill, the Indian houses, the rental office. "Think we can buy one here?"

"No. Maybe back up at Gold River."

Pulling out his keys, he said, "Well I guess we'd better get going."

Behind them a door slammed and Teddy turned to see a huge man, red-faced and familiar, standing on the fragile porch of the rental office.

"Steamboat?" she cried. "Is that you?"

Steamboat was wearing neatly ironed khakis and a jaunty Aussie hat. His girth was spanned by a down vest wide enough to upholster China. He squinted kindly. "You're Tabor's sister. I forgot your name."

"Teddy." She walked over. "What are you doing here?"

Gesturing to some folded orange tarps and scuba tanks at the bottom of the stairs, Steamboat said jubilantly, "Tabor called last night and asked if I could bring two airbags and some scuba tanks. You don't happen to know what she's diving for, do you?"

"Sort of." Teddy turned to Christian, who had ambled up beside her. "Christian, this is Steamboat Stevens, he wrestles on the same bill as my sister. Steamboat, this is Christian Wells."

Deftly dismounting the stairs, Steamboat shook hands with Christian, who asked, "You don't happen to have a chart, do you?"

Steamboat pointed to a blue pickup. "Yeah, in the truck."

"Great. Do you mind if we follow you out? We forgot to bring one."

"You going too?"

Teddy made a face. "My sister isn't known for her timidity."

The wrestler shrugged, shoulders heaving like uplifted hillsides. "Sure, you guys can follow. But first they have to find me a boat."

"You're renting one?" asked Teddy.

"I'm trying. They went to see if they could find one at the Indian reserve."

"Don't do that." She turned to Christian. "He can come with us, can't he?"

Christian ogled the giant. "My boat holds nine, max . . ."

"You guys work in pounds, don't you?" Steamboat plopped a hand on his chest. "I'm about three-fifty, these tanks," briskly he hefted one, "are about forty apiece . . ."

Christian paused to calculate. "Sounds okay. Go back in and tell them you don't need their boat."

"Great. Thanks."

Under Christian's careful eye, they delicately loaded the ski boat, balancing Steamboat across from the air tanks. Down the salty inlet they sped past craggy hillsides of fir, winding their way westward.

Steamboat pointed back off the stern. "You really want that line out there?"

Dragging behind the boat was fifty feet of yellow ski rope, plastic handle bouncing on the wake. Christian grimaced. "Oh, sh-oot. Teddy, could you grab that?"

Teddy leaned over the stern, and he turned to watch. "Careful. If it gets jammed in the propeller, we're dead in the water."

Teddy looped in the line, elbow to hand, and the icy water ran down her jacket. Her fingers were red with cold.

With only a windshield to hide behind, they unrolled sleeping bags and flung them over their shoulders. The hour was brutally long, the wind as relentless as a dental drill.

At the end of the channel ragged Bligh Island rose up

like Leviathan. Christian veered northward, leaving the accursed island to port. Rounding the point at Morgan Cove, they entered the little bay, gearing down to get their bearings.

"Amazing," said Teddy.

At the back of the cove March's shingled cottage floated dreamlike on bottle green. Behind the house was an extravagant hillside of hemlock, cedar, and fir—green as velvet, black as raven's eye.

Out from the storybook house came a man and woman waving broadly. Steamboat squinted and storm clouds passed over his face. "Who's that guy with Tabor?"

"Just some creep from Seattle." Teddy smiled encouragingly. "Don't worry. She beats him arm wrestling."

"Ahh."

They pulled in and Tabor grabbed their bow line. "Christian, Short Girl, are we glad to see you." Flatly she added, "Thanks for coming, Steamboat. I know that was short notice."

Teddy called, "What do you mean 'thanks for coming'? Did we have any choice?"

The front door opened and everyone fell silent. A formidable gray-haired woman strode out, clad in a fog-gray sweater. Her dark eyes gleamed slick as crowskin as she watched them offload. Teddy self-consciously hefted up the airbags and stepped over to the dock. Immediately she found herself face to face with Aurie, his eyes blurry with happiness. Seizing her hands and the airbags, he murmured, "Teddy, you came."

Icily, she disengaged her hands and gestured to Christian who unloaded scuba tanks. "Aurie, I'd like you to meet my friend Christian Wells. He's an experienced diver. Christian, this is Aurie Scholl, whom I was telling you about." Christian reached over to shake hands. "Glad to meet you. I hear you're diving alone."

Aurie stared at the elegant arch of Christian's cheekbones, barely missing a beat. "Yeah," he gestured to Tabor. "Wonder Woman's wetsuit is too small. If my insurance agent found out I was down there alone, he'd skin me with a dull knife."

"Definitely not good."

Tabor was in high spirits. "Who cares? We make a great team, don't we, Aurie? I didn't sink the boat, you didn't drown."

Aurie gave her an appreciative hug and Steamboat blurted painfully, "What are you guys looking for?"

March had come over to join the group, and Aurie introduced her to the newcomers—Teddy, Christian, and Steamboat. They smiled genially at the wildwoman, waiting for her response. "Will we be going back to Santa Gertrudis soon? I'd say we have two more hours of light."

Christian interjected, "Wait a minute. We need to know what's going on. What exactly are we supposed to bring up?"

Tabor held up Aurie's arm in triumph. "Aurie's found a treasure. Gold English guineas, we don't know how many. It belongs to March's family."

Teddy squealed. "You're kidding?"

Aurie pushed his glasses up his nose. "Actually, all I've found is a beat-to-hell iron forge." He gestured toward March. "Miss Hunt is the one who says it contains guineas."

"It does, Beamish. In the ash drawer. Why aren't we bringing it up right now?"

"Where is it?" Christian reached into his duffel and pulled out his black wetsuit and a nylon Speedo.

"I just told you," said March. "Santa Gertrudis Cove. Fifteen minutes from here."

"How deep?"

Aurie eyed Christian's sleek one-piece suit. "Twenty-five feet," he said. "The forge is just sitting there in the sand, big as a dishwasher. All we need is airbags to lift it with.''

"How do we know it won't fall apart on us?" Christian took off his overshirt and stuffed it in his duffel.

"Could," said Aurie. "But it looks pretty solid."

Holding up his gear, Christian looked around. "Anyplace we can change?"

March smiled with private pleasure. "Inside, Boy." She pointed a knobby finger at Teddy. "Are we going to put Hubert's other suit on the little one here?"

Tabor looked down at her sister. "That's a good idea. That'll put three of you guys down there."

Teddy backed away. "Oh, no. Not me."

"Teddy, please!"

"I haven't had a scuba tank on since P.E. The deep end of the Intramural pool is as serious as I get."

Halfway to the house, Christian stopped to examine the equipment propped against the wall. "Actually, Teddy," he picked up a buoyancy compensation vest, "this is an awfully good B.C. It would help a lot if you'd go down with us. All you'd have to do is hang out and give us your safe-second in case we get in trouble. Ever use one of these?"

Teddy shivered pitifully. "Can we go inside first?"

March growled. "Come on, all of you." She snatched up the air vest and led them into the store. Yanking several boxes of crackers off the shelf, she emptied them into a huge crockery bowl and set it on the cushioned window seat. "Keep talking, Boy. We don't want to lose the little one to the *sharks*."

Smiling, Christian grabbed a handful of crackers. "Don't pay any attention to her, Teddy. Look." He dangled the hand-held monitor that hung from the side of the vest. "This gives you readouts for depth, pressure, temperature, time under, remaining air." He punched a red button.

"Press here, you go up." The vest inflated. "Press here, you go down." The vest collapsed.

Teddy took a cracker. "The ones in college were never like this."

"An idiot can use these. And see?" He unhitched a second hose with mouthpiece attached to the bottom like a tail. "This is called the safe-second. You give it to your buddy if he gets in trouble. It's piped to your air."

"Wow."

"Yeah, and if we're only going twenty-five feet, you won't even have to decompress, just go down and come up slowly."

Steamboat turned suddenly. "What's that?"

Through the floorboards the prickly sound of a boat engine telegraphed from the water up into their bones. March bolted to the window. Seconds later the bow of a spectacular purple troller came around the point and she cried, "Bah! It's Bailley and his brats." Quickly she eyed her guests. "Not a word. Not a word. Bailley's here to find out why I borrowed the scuba gear, but we're going after my fish trap, you hear?"

They all peered out the window.

The fishing boat was high-tech and flashy with six antennae and a satellite dish on the mast. Whatever bulkhead surface was not custom-finished in pearlized lavender was heavily polished chrome. Standing in the doorway of the bridge was a handsome gray-haired Indian.

"He must do well," said Aurie.

"Bah! What's to do? His family has pulled fish out of the water for the last ten thousand years."

Tabor read from the wind guard of the flying bridge: " '*Nuu-chal-nulth Maid.*' What's Nuu-chal-nulth?"

"It's what the Nootka are calling themselves this year. 'People of the west mountains.' Pay no attention, they're fighting among themselves. They'll be something else next year."

Christian put down the gear. "I'll go help him dock."

"Stay here, Boy. He wouldn't know what to do with you."

Still thirty feet from the float Bailley cut the engine. As the troller glided in, he deftly hopped off the bow and wrapped a bowline around a midships cleat. Interrupted in its forward progress, the boat sprung sideways toward the dock. As it drifted the last few feet, Bailley caught stern lines thrown by three black-haired boys and wrapped them aft. The boys leaped off in turn and waited respectfully while Bailley finished docking. Only when he was ready to proceed did they follow him into the store.

"Mr. Bailley!" March gushed. "How are you? Why boys, you're growing like weeds. So *good* to see my neighbors. What can I do for you?"

The boys spotted Steamboat and promptly huddled around their grandfather, their mouths open. Steamboat was a khaki mountain in a roomful of midgets.

With greatest aplomb Steamboat quietly settled himself down on the window seat, reducing his bulk by half. He smiled at the boys. "Hi, guys, how you doin'?"

The boys relaxed, the threat instantly passed.

"Well, Bailley," said March. "What's up?"

Bailley had high coastal cheekbones burnished like elk hide, and a flat polished nose the color of honey. In a quiet monotone, he replied, "Edith ran out of Bisquick and we're not going to Gold River for another week."

March scurried to the shelf. "Bisquick. Bisquick we have."

"Grandpa?"

Bailley dug into his pockets and showered the boys with change. "None of that purple stuff now."

The boys charged the candy shelf as if sucked by gravity. As the crowd of adults watched in amusement, Bailley commented softly, "Mrs. Hubert said you borrowed the scuba gear."

"She didn't tell you? I lost my fish trap." March gestured to the crowd around the window seat. "My friends here are going to help me."

Aurie stepped forward, hand outstretched. "How do you do? I'm Aurie Scholl." The men shook hands and Aurie said, "And this is Teddy and Tabor Morelli." He hesitated. ". . . and some friends."

"Umm."

March broke in. "I forgot introductions. Friends, this is my neighbor John Bailley from Yuquot, and these are his grandsons. The Bailleys have lived at Friendly Cove for over ten thousand years, far as anybody can tell. But they weren't the Bailleys back then, were they?"

Aurie whistled. "You know that your family has lived there the whole time?"

Bailley's low Nootka voice settled like evening. "That's what they say."

March effused. "The archaeologists have only gone down four thousand years, but the midden looks to be about ten thousand years old, isn't that right, Mr. Bailley?"

"Umm." He called to the oldest boy and said something in Nootka that caused the child to disappear outside. "We heard about your sister down there in Washington. I'm real sorry that happened."

"What happens, happens, Bailley."

He turned to Tabor and Teddy. "One of you telephone to bring up the dolls?"

Tabor touched her chest. "I did. I used to rent a room from Margaret."

"Margaret was a nice lady."

"Yes, she was."

Eyeing March, he said pointedly, "*Margaret* really cared about the Nuu-chal-nulth people getting what was theirs."

March held out the Bisquick. "Now, now, Mr. Bailley, let's not confuse 'the people' with 'the Bailleys.' I believe the politburo used to have the same problem." She furrowed her brow. "Will that be all you need?"

The third boy came back inside and eyed his grandfather. Satisfied, Bailley pulled Canadian bills from a zippered pouch. "I think that'll do it. Thank you very much." Clutching his box of Bisquick, he turned to the newcomers while March made change. "Guess we better let you get on with your diving. Not much daylight left. Come by the house if you need anything."

"Good*bye*, Mr. Bailley," March said. She crinkled her face at the boys, and cooed, "Goodbye, boys. Such *nice* boys. Come again."

The Bailleys started up the boat and March immediately put on her waders. Aurie said, "Your fish trap doesn't happen to be in the shed, does it?"

"The shed!" She rushed to the window. "He sent his brat into my shed. Now he'll be watching."

Tabor unzipped a duffel to look at the scuba gear. "If it's legally your treasure, why are you worried about him?"

"Legal? Who knows what's legal? Bailley thinks just because his ancestors were here, he owns the whole place. Did you hear that blather? 'The people.' Bah!"

As the sound of the troller grew fainter in their bones, Teddy unlaced her shoes. "But won't he be watching us?"

"The only good thing about that floating whorehouse of his, is he can't sneak up anywhere. We'll anchor your ski boat with the diving flag down at the far end of my cove to look like we're diving for the fish trap. Then we can take the other two rigs 'round Bligh to the north and slip into Gertrudis that way. Bailley won't come in here to spy, he's too proud."

Christian unlaced his boots. "That might work. Only thing is, we need to leave a person in your runabout so it looks like somebody is monitoring the divers."

"Bah. That's no problem. I'll find you a person." March

opened the bottom cabinet and dragged out a fifty-pound sack of flour. Peeling off her furry sweater, she draped it over the flour sack. "There she is. There she is. How's that for a person?"

9

"Okay," March croaked. "Let's see how fast we can get this done." She ripped three holes in a black trash bag and slipped it on over her head.

They watched open-mouthed as she hopped into her runabout and towed Christian's skiboat to the end of the cove, leaving it piloted by the flour sack. Waiting for her return, everyone began settling into Aurie's sturdy pilothouse and stowing gear. When March got back Tabor was still on the dock and Steamboat dashed out of the aluminun pilothouse, holding up an arm. "Here, Tabor, hop in." Tabor ignored him and climbed into the other boat with March.

Following March up Hanna Channel, Aurie whistled gamely through his teeth, tracking cautiously around the northern shoals of Bligh. Steamboat sized up Aurie's defective muscle tone, unable to make heads or tails of this new situation. "You from Tabor's old gym in Seattle?"

Gleefully Aurie raked his hand through his hair. "Alas, nothing quite that exotic. I'm an orthopedic surgeon." He steered into one of the glossy channels of March's wake.

"What'd you say your name was?" asked Steamboat.

"Aurelian Scholl. Aurie."

"What?"

"Sorry. Nothing I can do about it."

"You aren't related to the Foot Doctor Scholl, are you?"

Aurie pushed his glasses up his nose. "Ah, sadly, no. I'm afraid the only claim to fame I can make is through my paternal great-great-grandfather and namesake, Parisian inventor Aurelian Scholl. A brilliant man, really." Merrily, his eyes glinted. "You remember what he did, of course?"

Steamboat shook his head. "No."

"Why, Grandpapa Aurelian was the inventor of the rubber newspaper, especially designed to be read in the bathtub. A man before his time."

Steamboat eyed him cautiously. "I don't know whether you're kidding or not."

"I know." Aurie's face dropped. "No one ever does. Teddy my sweet, could you explain to Steamboat about the Second Empire?"

Frostily, Teddy narrowed her eyes. "Published any articles lately, Aurie?"

Aurie stared through the windshield. "Not a one, my dear."

Addressing the group, Teddy continued, "Aurie had the great good fortune as a fourth-year med student to have his Isthmus project published in *Annals of Athletic Medicine.* It was about the beginnings of the sports medicine movement in nineteenth-century Germany. Isn't that right, Aurie?"

Aurie mumbled.

"It seems that Aurie's committee was very impressed, not only with his historical understanding, but also with the fact that he translated articles like *'Verletzungen beim Wintersport: Erfahrungen im Oberengadin'* from old German medical journals." Solicitously she asked, "Did you find that tedious, Aurie?"

There was an icy silence and Christian asked, "Are we missing something here?"

Keeping his eyes on March's wake, Aurie huffed, "I used her research. She was doing it for a History of Science seminar anyway."

They were silent for the rest of the trip until they reached a gap in the hills where March geared down while swerving starboard. "Is this Santa Gertrudis?" asked Steamboat.

"Sure is," answered Aurie.

From a narrow cleft the cove spread out into twin bays dotted with rugged rocks and shoals. They opened the door to the little cabin and were instantly whacked by winter chill. The late afternoon mist had condensed to light mizzle and everyone except the divers zipped and wrapped whatever they had not done up before. March anchored near some craggy bird-stained islets and Aurie followed, lashing his midships to March's plywood gunnels.

"It's directly below," said March.

Teddy peered over the side. Three feet down baitfish hovered ambivalently, wondering whether to dart to safety or hang around for the excitement. The drizzle made pin-sized dimples on the sheen, giving the surface the appearance of gooseflesh. Tabor hopped from March's boat and looked over too, her reflection joining Teddy's on the surface. "I wish I could go down."

Overheated by the double layer of rubber coat and Farmer John's, Teddy unzipped her jacket. "I still don't understand why we're doing this."

March called over while setting a second anchor from her bow. "We're diving for treasure and you ask why?"

Christian touched Teddy lightly on the waist. "Stand up and we'll strap on a tank."

She stood and they latched the yellow cylinder on her back. Then for the next fifteen minutes they all buckled, zipped, and velcroed the rest of the equipment, adding thirty pounds to their body weight. They tested valves, blew into pipes, and filled their vests with air. Clad in her trash bag, March sat swinging the bitter end of her docking line to keep the gulls from fouling her decks.

Finally Christian was ready. Lowering the orange airbags overboard on a weighted line, he perched himself on the gunnels and spit into his mask, coating the glass to keep it from fogging. Filling his B.C. slightly, he leaned backward, holding the mask against his face. "Okay, everybody, day's not getting any longer." He lifted legs and landed with a splash, treading to wait for the others. Aurie repeated the act, mimicking every gesture. Then it was Teddy's turn.

Fitting on her mask, she jetted a little air into her vest and sat on the gunnels, nudging herself back slowly.

"Just go, Teddy."

She fell with a splash. "*Yooow!*" Cold clubbed her cheekbones like a car wreck. Frigid water burned her spine.

Christian splashed happy as a polar bear. "You'll get used to it. Come on, let's go."

Pressing air release valves on their vests, they sank down through the green haze, searching the glaucous depths for a bottom. Teddy's sinuses felt like they were filled with hot lead, and every sudden movement saturated her slightly-warmed suit with acid-cold water. The only sound was her breathing: Darth Vader's ominous sucking in, her own happy bubbles blowing out.

Learning to make slow movements to keep the cold at bay, she held her nose and blew as pressure mounted in her ears. Visibility was barely five feet.

An eel darted through the jade soup, as did a transparent jellyfish the size of a plate. Moments later the bottom came into view, a sloping plain of caramel-colored sand, empty except for a neat row of black stubs racked out as regularly as fence posts. They touched down and Teddy swam over behind the men, who had raced to the stubs. Thrusting her own face closely toward one of the tips, she saw that it was a piece of bloated black lumber. She peered down the row of stubs as it disappeared into the murk and realized she was looking at the ribs of an antique sailing vessel.

Aurie urged them on through the haze. Finning past the stubs, they came to a ravaged black heap covered with barnacles. Christian broke off a knobby bit and crumbled it in his glove. The forge was as fragile as sugar cookies. Pantomiming to Aurie and Teddy to dig with their hands under the heap, Christian swam over to the liftbags he had lowered before the dive.

Aurie touched Teddy's arm for attention and enacted a little pantomime to show that they should scoop tunnels starting from either side of the forge and meet in the middle. Christian came back to help and the three of them dug for fifteen minutes, working holes in their gloves and breaking off pieces of the crumbly forge every time they bumped their foreheads.

After a while Christian tapped on Teddy's gauge and showed her tank was down to 500 psi's. He jerked his thumb topside and she nodded, waving goodbye.

Inflating her vest from the regulator, she whisked to the surface, popping high out of the water into plain, thin air.

"Teddy! Over here."

Turning around, she paddled to the boats, and threw her fins into the aluminum rental. She climbed the ladder, and was greeted by Tabor, Steamboat, and March, spring-loaded with questions.

"You find it?"

"Yes."

"Your nose is bleeding. You came up too fast."

She wiped her nose and unzipped her jacket, already too warm.

"Well?" asked Tabor.

She perched on the cockpit seat. "It's the forge, all right. It's really big, though. I don't know how we're going to lift it."

"With the airbags, dummy."

"No." Teddy shook her head. "I mean once they float it to the surface, how are we going to get it into the boat?"

March fabricated a smile and laid a hand on a tall gin pole plugged into the stern of Aurie's boat. "I brought my hoist, dearie. I've been planning this for a long time."

Shackled to the gin pole was an ancient wooden block and tackle.

''Where are the guys?'' asked Tabor.

''I don't know. I thought they'd be out of air too.''

March chided, ''No, they sent you up early. You didn't know how to use your air.''

Teddy dried her face and they all watched patiently as huge bubbles erupted on the surface, like the welling of a spring. After a few minutes March rearranged her black trash bag and said abruptly, ''Sir, back to my birds; if you sauté the duck breast with mushrooms, where do the apples and curry come in?''

Teddy looked around to see whom March was addressing so decorously.

''Oh,'' said Steamboat. ''You need a different saucepan for that. You want to dice the apples and soften them in a little butter.'' Unconsciously he held up a forefinger to indicate one ''knuckle'' of butter. ''Then add a little grated onion. Move that around on medium heat, sprinkle in flour, a good curry powder, salt and pepper. Heat. Deglaze with cream, Madeira, and duck stock—chicken broth will do. Warm it all up, *then* add the duck and mushrooms.'' He shrugged his shoulders. ''Serve over rice.''

''How long were you a cook?'' asked Tabor reverently.

''Whole time I was in National Service. They saw on my résumé I'd done cooking lessons in Toulouse and they didn't realize it was only a bogus way of taking university French. So basically, I had to learn everything right before I cooked it. They'd come in: 'General wants to know if you can do Partridge Drouant?' 'Sure, no problem.' So I'd race over to the library and find out what Partridge Drouant was.''

With bated breath, Tabor asked, ''What's Partridge Drouant?''

''Birds, tangerine, Madeira. Basically the whole gourmet thing works on Madeira—Madeira and cream. They let me have anything I wanted so I always ordered top of the line.'' He shook his head. ''It was a crazy job.''

''And before that you went to U.B.C.,'' March insisted.

''That's right.''

''And I bet there's something else you want to tell us, isn't there, sir?''

Startled, Steamboat silenced March, his rusty eyelashes blinking.

''Oh, well. All in good time.''

Huge crystal bubbles welled from the depths and they all peered over, spying a faint orange haze far below. ''They're coming,'' cried Tabor.

''Make way, make way,'' said March. She swung the gin pole around until the arm hung over the side.

The orange bags popped high out of the water, then settled back as the black-hooded divers burst up immediately behind. Lowering the steely hook to the water, March called, ''Bring it around to this side.''

Christian and Aurie towed the air bags over as March trembled in feverish anticipation. Christian called, ''Slow down, everybody. Let's do this right.''

They strapped the lines from the forge onto March's hook, and before Christian and Aurie could even swim around to the ladder, March was hoisting up the pulley, with Steamboat standing by ineffectually. The crumbly black heap rose from the sea and sluiced like a fountain. March cackled.

Steamboat leaned over and guided the dripping hulk into the cockpit, while Teddy examined the crumbly pile in the clear light of day. Gray barnacles welded so tightly onto the corroded metal they were impossible to pull off without snapping off chunks of iron. Down in the caved-in center of the forge, a fuzzy turquoise object lay sunken in a pond of seawater.

''The ash drawer's on the bottom,'' barked March. ''Hold it up for me, sir.''

Aurie and Christian boarded the boat like latecomers to a party as Steamboat knelt down and lifted the forge. Carefully laying it on its side, he moved back, soaking wet. March clawed at the exposed bottom of the hulk. "Bah! Give me a rod or something."

Christian unstrapped his diving knife and presented it to her, handle first. Grabbing the knife, she chipped off bits of crumbly iron, peppering the deck with black frizzle. Finally she sat up. "I can't find it. It's not there. Maybe the other side."

Aurie peered down into the caved-in interior of the forge. "You know, I think that curved thing inside is the handle of something." He pointed to a furry turquoise half-moon. "It's covered with copper salts."

Christian squinted in. "I think you're right. Mind if we pull it out, March?"

"Pull."

With the help of the knife, they slowly teased out the handle and, attached to it, an entire bucket-shaped object, leprous with copper mold.

"What do you know," said Tabor. "An old-fashioned copper bucket. But what's it doing inside the forge? Wouldn't it melt?"

Teddy pulled off her hood and stretched her neck. "I don't think it's a bucket, per se. The Royal Navy used to cook in these and I assume the merchant marine did too. I've seen them on display at the Maritime Museum." She looked at Christian, trying to understand. "So how would a cooking pot end up inside a forge?"

"Maybe it settled there when it sunk."

"Yeah," agreed Tabor. "Things must have floated around before the ship hit bottom."

Silently they let the thought sink in.

"Noooo!" March's sudden scream echoed like the cry of a gull. Stiff with rage, she screamed again. "You bloody fools! This isn't the bloody forge. This is the bloody cookstove!"

10

Christian squinted at the worsted gray sky. "It's too late to go down again. We don't even know where to look."

"Well, I guess that's that." Aurie pulled off his hood and looked at his watch. "Maybe we can make Gold River before dark."

"No!" Rigid with anger, March clamped the pulley lines around the rotting stove. "You can't make Gold River before dark. Besides, the forge is still *sitting* there! You just didn't look for it, did you, Beamish? Grabbed on to the first thing you found."

Aurie stared at the air tank between his legs.

"You're all coming back to my house for supper, then we can decide what to do. Cookie," she barked to Steamboat, "help me toss this over. Girlie, untie the boats."

Too hungry to protest, the recruits did as they were told while Aurie, Teddy, and Christian cleaned up diving gear. Sorting themselves into two boats for the ride back to Morgan Cove, they tied up at the floating cottage where March pulled off her trash bag and again began bawling orders. "You, Cookie," she called to Steamboat, "there's live rockfish in the pen behind my sheds. Think you can do something with them?"

"Sure," said Steamboat.

"Freddy!"

Teddy stopped dead in her tracks. "Yes, ma'am?"

"On the racks in the smaller shed are potatoes and onions. Sniff out the rotten ones and throw them in the cove. Then bring Cookie a big handful of both."

"Yes, ma'am."

"Beamish, you help Girlie and Christian get this mess off my float. I can't *stand* all this clutter mucking up the place."

Stunned to silence, they all performed their tasks as March piloted down to Christian's ski boat and towed the flour sack dummy home. Teddy brought an armful of vegetables to Steamboat, who was watching Christian snare rockfish with a wide-mouthed net. Cornering one finally, Christian held it up and they watched the ugly red fish flap inside the mesh. "Want me to dress it for you, Steamboat?"

"That'd be great." Steamboat held his fingers about one inch apart. "Sort of thick fillets with a pocket sliced in?"

"Fine."

Aurie called from across the dock. "Teddy, I could use some extra hands hosing off equipment."

She glanced over quickly, then said, "Sorry, I'm helping Christian with the fish." She turned to him. "I've never filleted before, may I try?"

"Be my guest."

They all worked busily for twenty minutes, gradually finding themselves lured inside by transcendent smells from the kitchen. Standing in front of the great Monarch stove with a blue-checked dishtowel across his chest, Steamboat deftly mixed sautéed onions, crabmeat, and breadcrumbs for stuffing. Packing the mixture into rockfish fillets, he cinched them with marjoram twigs plucked from March's rafters. Beside him Tabor deferentially mashed potatoes to be "duchessed" around the fish through a waxed paper funnel.

A phone rang and both Aurie and Christian lurched for

their duffels. "Mine," said Christian. He raised the antenna and punched "receive," taking the phone outside to the darkening air.

Teddy watched his retreating back, then—following March's example—poured herself a mug of hot water over dried raspberry leaves. Leaning against the counter, she asked, "Steamboat, why aren't you cooking professionally?"

Tabor looked up from the potatoes, also anxious to hear the reply.

Steamboat shrugged. "I don't want to get started on that restaurant thing, gets too crazy. What I'd really like to do is cook in a hunting lodge in the Yukon."

"The Yukon?"

"Used to fish there with my dad—cook summers, wrestle winters, wouldn't that be the life? That way I could drop some of this weight, at least part of the year."

Christian came back inside, looking irritable and distracted.

"Is everything okay?" asked Teddy.

"No, Angela's in town. The funeral home wants her to sign a waiver saying they received the body with a broken nose."

"How'd that happen?"

"How should I know?" Christian shrugged, perplexed. "All I can think of is that the paramedics dropped him and don't want to admit it. I told her go ahead and sign."

Teddy rubbed a finger across her chin. "Or maybe, too, they didn't like the way he bit through his bottom lip with his teeth."

"Anyway, Angela wants me back in town." Christian looked expectantly at March. "I told her I'd be there tomorrow night."

March ignored him.

Aurie stood gloomily in the doorway between the kitchen and store. "Teddy, can I talk to you for a minute?"

"What for?"

"Please."

Clutching her tea mug, she followed him outside into the dark chill. Aurie leaned against a dock post, tucking his hands into his pockets and gazing wistfully into her eyes. "You looked adorable in your little wetsuit today."

"Thank you."

"I still can't believe all the adult bodily functions are packed into such a small unit. Teddy Morelli: distilled essence of woman."

She pressed her lips together. She was just an inch taller than Jennifer. "Aurie, what do you want?"

"Just to see how you are. Tabor told me about the other night; you've had a pretty rough week, haven't you?"

"Understatement."

"Listen." He propped his foot on the low railing. "I know you're under a lot of stress right now, but don't you think you're leaning on the wrong people for support? I mean, later on you've got this heavy transfer thing to deal with."

"Aurie, I haven't a clue what you're talking about."

"Never mind." He glanced to the lighted window. "How did March know Steamboat could cook?"

"They were talking in the boat. Which reminds me, were you there when March acted like he'd done something?"

"Like what?"

"I don't know. They both shut up right away."

"You don't mean like killing Margaret?"

"No." She shook her head. "Nothing like that. I want to ask Tabor what she thought of it."

Aurie gazed in the window again. Tabor and Christian were noisily slapping each other's hands in a reflex-testing game; Tabor was killing him. "You might also do Tabor a favor and find out how her Margaret Zimmerman got the map in the first place. We still don't know if March has any claim to salvage rights. Or if she killed her sister to get them.''

Teddy shook her head. ''No, I thought of that. March couldn't have killed her because she had no way to get down there. The runabout's her only transportation.''

''I'm still worried about you, though.''

She looked him in the eye. ''What about me?''

''I guess I want to warn you away from the Baby Macho in there. This isn't anything serious, is it?''

She clenched her jaw. ''His name is Christian, Aurie. And the answer is that it's as serious as he wants to make it.''

''God, Teddy, he's so shallow. You don't even need galoshes to wade through that.''

''Well, my goodness! Aurie Scholl is jealous. I'm surprised you've even noticed there're other people on the planet.''

''I'm not jealous. I just want you to take a good look at him. He's in there playing Wilderness Yuppie of the North and the only reason we're not laughing our heads off is that he's wearing a textbook pair of zygomatic arches. Pretty counts for *nothing,* Teddy. Didn't you learn anything from my experience?''

''Stop it, you're embarrassing yourself.'' She poured her cold tea into the cove and started toward the house.

Blocking her path, he said, ''Look, what do I have to do to make you see how unproductive all this is? I'm not even going to mention his age.''

''Aurie, I'm telling you, stay away.''

He stepped back, suddenly amiable. He pushed his glasses up his nose. ''Okay. If that's how it is, I guess I'll just have to talk to the boy myself, see if his intentions are honorable.''

Teddy gritted her teeth, breathing hate. ''Aurie, so help me, if you do your arrogant Seattle orthopod thing, I'll never speak to you again.''

"I don't do arrog..." Aurie crossed his arms and looked out into the dark. "Okay, then. Teddy Morelli and the Pretty Idiot. Must be something that happens to us as we age."

She narrowed her eyes. "Yeah, I did notice your hair was turning gray. You'll have to tell me about it sometime: little scary? Does that work something like a wakeup call?" She brushed past. "Which reminds me: did you know that your grandmother's writing table is a nineteenth-century reproduction? Christian said there are only two genuine Boulle pieces in existence and I got the impression they're both in museums."

The meal was superb. The flaky white fillets yielded up their bounty with the scratch of a fork. Savory potato rosettes graced the rim of the platter, crusty on the outside, meltingly smooth within. To balance the offering, Steamboat added canned peas from the store shelves sautéed with onions and mint. For dessert he served up packaged angel cake smothered with hot sabayon sauce made from March's blackberry wine.

Afterwards they all sat around the kitchen, drinking mugs of raspberry tea. Aurie fidgeted restlessly, slamming his mug against the table without meaning to, while March hummed in a corner, her legs crossed under her long skirt, one sturdy hiking boot keeping private rhythm.

"Well," she said finally. "One quick dive first thing in the morning, you can all be out of here by noon."

Christian wiped his mouth with one of her blue embroidered napkins and tucked it next his plate. "March, there's a rule of three in diving: it takes three times as long as you think, and costs three times as much."

"But the forge is right there, just under the sand! All you have to do is use the metal detector. Beamish didn't even take it with him last time."

"All I'm saying is that these things take time."

"March." Aurie leaned against the kitchen counter. "Has it occurred to you that if you actually take salvage from this shipwreck, you're going to get in trouble with the authorities? Local governments are very touchy about what belongs to whom."

"No problem there, Beamish. This one's mine."

Aurie gulped his tea and brought the mug to the sink. "I'm sure that's easy to say. But all we know is that your sister had a purloined map."

March curled her lip. "Such an ugly word. Sit down and I'll tell you why it's mine." She picked up a poker and opened the firebox of the huge black Monarch. Rearranging the faggots, her eyes looked past the flames to the place where stories were kindled. "Okay, Dearie. The story begins in the summer of 1802 in Hull, England. Are you ready?"

"What?"

"Beamish, I told you to sit down."

Aurie lowered himself onto a chair as everyone in the room watched the crazy black-eyed woman stoke her range.

Closing the firebox, March began: "Now, in the town of Hull in 1802 the young blacksmith John Jewitt happened to make ship on the American brigantine *Boston*. The *Boston* was in port undergoing repairs and taking on English manufactured goods to trade at Nootka Sound. It seems that the captain of the *Boston* took a liking to young Jewitt and thought a blacksmith might be useful on board. Jewitt's father, the master smithy who was doing repairs on the boat, encouraged his son to go and set him up with a portable forge and a certain sum of money to be laid out for the sea otter trade, which was very lucrative at the time."

"Oh," said Tabor. "Teddy was telling us about that."

"Good. Good. Ever heard of Maquinna?"

They all shook their heads.

"Well, the chief at Friendly Cove at the time was a clever old bird named Maquinna. He had been wined and dined royally by Europeans back earlier when the English and Spanish were bickering over the place, then summarily ignored. Feeling like he had been snubbed one time too many—and maybe just getting too greedy—he decided he needed to strike back at the Europeans. So, one fine April day in 1803 when the *Boston* had laid anchor in Friendly Cove, he led his men in a surprise attack, massacring everyone on board and keeping the ship's cargo for himself. It was a very clever plan, worked like a charm, except that young Jewitt and another old seadog named Thompson ended up down below and didn't get killed. Jewitt was made prisoner, but didn't even know if he wanted to live because the first thing Maquinna did was cut the heads off all the crew, line them up on the ship's rail, then make Jewitt identify them.''

''Ugh.''

''To make a long story short, Jewitt was quick-witted enough to ingratiate himself with Maquinna by blacksmithing. Halibut hooks, knife blades, harpoons. He impregnated a native wife, and after two years, finally tricked Maquinna into letting him and Thompson leave on a passing ship.''

''When's this?'' asked Teddy. ''1805 or so?''

''Exactly,'' said March.

Aurie said, ''I guess the *Boston* was too big for Jewitt and Thompson to have escaped in by themselves?''

March looked at him keenly. ''Don't rush ahead. That's the part we're coming to.'' March crossed her arms, tucking her gnarly hands into the folds of the sweater. ''At any rate, right after the attack, Maquinna forced Jewitt and the Indians to sail the *Boston* up the coast and beach it. For almost two hundred years people have been searching for the ship, all around Boston Point. It's a *grand* joke, d'you see? They named it 'Boston' Point to throw us off the scent. Wouldn't be surprised if old Maquinna named the point himself.

''Where were we? Oh, yes. So after the ship was beached—in Santa Gertrudis, eh?—Maquinna and his boys looted the ship for three days and nights, until finally a lone native pilfering in the dark dropped his torch in the hold and burned the ship 'til it sank.''

Teddy said softly, ''But how do you know there are guineas in the wreck, March?''

She stood. ''Let me get Jewitt's journal. It's easier to explain.'' Mounting an open stairway at the back of the kitchen, she climbed halfway to a bedroom loft and plucked a book from built-in shelves. Descending seconds later, she held out an antique green volume. Embossed on the spine was gold Gothic type: ''The Jewitt Narrative.'' On the cover Victorian script swirled like filigree.

Leafing pages, March said, ''In his journal Jewitt tells about the financial arrangements he made with the captain before he sailed. It's right here somepl— Ah, yes: 'My father consented that I should ship on board the *Boston* as an armorer, at the rate of thirty dollars per month, with an agreement that the amount due me—together with a certain sum of money which my father gave Capt. Salter for the purpose—should be laid out by him on the Northwest Coast in the purchase of furs on my account . . .' ''

''*Thirty* dollars?'' Tabor screwed up her face.

''No, Girlie. Wait.'' March flipped pages. ''Now further on, Jewitt describes his workplace on the ship: 'I found myself well accommodated on board as regarded my work, an iron forge having been erected on deck; this my father had made for the ship on a new plan; while a corner of the steerage was appropriated to my vise bench, so that in bad weather I could work below.'

''Now.'' March rested the book on her thigh. ''It doesn't say so in the journal, but I happen to know that the amount Jewitt's father gave him for the fur trade was fifty gold guineas.''

''How do you know?'' asked Aurie.

March ignored him. ''What's more, it's not public knowledge, but I also know, that after everyone else was killed, and Jewitt was taking his smithing tools off the boat, he cracked the captain's safe and took not only his fifty guineas, but *all* the money in the till to keep it away from the looting Indians. At that point, I would have done the same, would you have?''

''No. How'd he hide it in a burning forge?''

''Just a minute, you need to know something else first. As I told you, after the attack, Jewitt ingratiated himself quite well with Maquinna and one of the things Maquinna did to make Jewitt more amenable to staying was arrange a marriage for him with a young girl named Eustochee–exqua, daughter of Upquesta. It was not a happy situation for Jewitt—he was a perfectly healthy young man, but his agreeing to marry was the same as agreeing to stay permanently—and just about the time Jewitt tricked Maquinna into letting him leave on the visiting brig *Lydia,* Eustochee revealed that she was pregnant. As is not surprising, Jewitt expressed no regret about quitting his native wife to go back to civilization.

''But,'' March paused, waiting for her listeners, ''Jewitt's conscience must have gotten the better of him, because before he left, he told Eustochee that his King George money and a great stash of Boston money was in the ash drawer of his forge in the sunken ship. He said that if there was ever a *very* low tide, she might try to recover this money and use it in trading with the Europeans.

''Of course Jewitt was mistaken about the tide—it never gets that low—but for the past eight generations the descendants of Eustochee's son have told their children the story about the 'King George's money' and the 'Boston money'—American money—that Jewitt hid. In each generation they've been very careful to pass on the exact location of the ship in case there ever was that low tide Jewitt was waiting for.''

''And now there's a map of it?'' asked Aurie.

''Yes.''

Tabor looked at the map for a moment, then said, "But March, the money doesn't belong to you. Like Aurie said, even if you can evade the family, the government of British Columbia isn't going to let you walk away with whatever you find."

"No, Girlie, let me show you something." March stood up and reached onto a rafter, knocking drying herbs to the floor. Unwrapping a greasy brown cloth, she held out a primitive steel knife, blue-black, with a wickedly thin blade. Its fat handle was wrapped with tarry string.

"What is it?" said Aurie.

"Jewitt made this from a shovel. Polished it up for Eustochee as a filleting knife." She tested it with her thumb. "I like to keep it honed."

"Where'd *you* get it?"

"My father's kitchen."

"And where'd he get it?"

"You still don't understand, do you?" March rewrapped the knife. "My father was Nootka, or at least part Nootka. Margaret and I happen to be the only living descendants of the child fathered by Jewitt and Eustochee." She held up her bony fingers and counted. "John Jewitt is my great-great-great-great-great-great-grandfather. I can recite the genealogy if you like."

11

Everyone sat silent.

Tabor scribbled in the rich purple dessert sauce with her fork. "March, that's an incredible story, but you know what you haven't told me yet? You said you have some information about who killed Margaret."

March stretched her face into a smile. "I haven't told you because you haven't brought up my forge."

Teddy leaned forward. "Oh, and Tabor also said you knew some Chinook . . ."

March stood, removing plates. "That's right. I'll write it all down tomorrow while you're diving. Give me something to do."

Teddy picked up plates to follow. "You know March, it would be much easier to dive for you if you were a little more forthcoming about what's going on here. I mean, it's really hard to know if we're doing the right thing . . ."

March puckered her mouth. "Well, it would be no great loss if you stayed topside, would it, Freddy?"

Tabor leaned forward in her chair. "March, I think all of us would like to know why you think you should get Jewitt's money. I mean, you just said the Jewitt story was always passed on orally, but here you had to have a map. And what bothers me even more is that you think Margaret was hiding it from you. That's not like her."

123

March scratched the back of her hand. "Margaret was hiding it because Margaret wanted to keep it all herself."

Tabor shook her head. "I don't think so. The more I think about it, the more I think she didn't even know she had the map. I mean, the suitcase was out in the barn, and knowing Margaret—I mean—why wasn't she writing a book about it? Little kids and buried treasure? That'd be right up her alley."

March grimaced. "She was writing about something else. A flood on the river down there, Cookshack, Rucksack."

"Nooksack?"

"That's it. The flood of '51. Her neighbor lady was twelve years old at the time, ended up with a dead horse in her bedroom."

"A flood?" Tabor's eyes widened. "Why would somebody steal computer disks about a flood?"

"Bah." March's eyes flared. "Somebody was bound to do her in. I can't be the only person in the world who loathes a charlatan and a liar."

Tabor snapped her head as if slapped. "I'm sorry. I don't believe that for a moment. I think Margaret was a remarkable woman."

"No, no, Girlie, let's call things what they are: Margaret was a charlatan, a thief, and a liar."

Tabor folded her troubled arms over her chest. "I can't listen to this. It makes no sense to me."

March sneered. "How much did Margaret tell you about us?"

"Nothing really."

"Did she ever tell you about our mother, our appalling childhood?"

"No."

March sat down again. "I'm surprised she didn't reinvent the whole story for you, with herself playing Queen Boadicea." She picked up the poker and glanced around the room. "Okay, dearies, you asked for it."

She stared through the blurry mica window of the firebox into the golden light beyond. "What you need to know is that our mother was a Strachan from Toronto. You've never heard of them, you're American. Strachans trace their roots back to the early days of Upper Canada: Tories, Family Compact, blah, blah, on and on. Our mother was an only child, both willful and spoiled, beautiful and ignored; one of the few early women radicals at University of Toronto.

"After graduation in 1932 Mother broke off with her family and took the train out to the great Pacific Unknown to write adventure stories for *Maclean's* magazine. She bought herself a converted fishing boat to live on, chugged up and down the coast reveling and drinking, leaving scandal in her wake. Meanwhile, back in Ontario, she developed quite a following in *Maclean's* as the plucky little heroine of her own stories. Of course, they had no idea of the reality.

"One of Mother's favorite turns, for instance, was to bang about, only woman upwoods in a lumber camp, then chug back down to Victoria Harbor, tie up when the legislature convened. She would sit at high tea in the Empress Hotel, chumming about with M.P.s, laughing at them behind their backs. Mother said she always loved contrasts. For a while she tried to run with Emily Carr, the painter, but Miss Carr had the good sense to avoid Mother like the plague.

"Needless to say," March hugged her bony arms, "the woman made a terrible mother. She met our father—an artist, half-Nootka, whose family traced its lines back to both Jewitt *and* Maquinna—down at the Provincial Museum where he was helping set up the early Nootka displays, trying to explain to the befuddled curators that the word 'Nootka' was not the name of his father's people, but only Captain Cook's misunderstanding of the Indians' re-

quest to '*nootka icim*.' " She drew a circle in the air:
" 'Come on around to the harbor.' "

"Madness." She shook her head. "At any rate, my parents were madly attracted by their differences and had a quick passionate affair in which Mother got pregnant. They married, found immediately that they couldn't live together, and that children cramped mother's style. After a few years Father found a way to be always off fishing, and Mother dragged us back and forth between here and Toronto, alternately renouncing and making up with her family. No matter where we were, she summarily ignored us, as she tried to peck out the great Canadian novel on the typewriter."

March stopped for a moment, opening the firebox and suddenly closing it again. "Now I know this sounds like the rantings of a bitter old woman, but you must understand the situation: the profound unsuitability of this woman as a mother, and our alternating childhood realities: on the one hand, being treated like pitiful little half-breeds back in Toronto, and on the other, scavenging dumb animals in the B.C. woods. I've seen Mother's *Maclean's* stories and the fraudulence was appalling. As she portrayed it, this was a life of charming poverty—tiny cabins, drawn water, freezing rooms in winter—but for a child, it was all *unspeakably* real.

"I remember getting into beds so cold we cried ourselves to sleep. Diapers, of course, had to be washed by hand, and mother was so little interested she let Margaret develop permanent scars from diaper rash. My most vivid memory of childhood is huddling inside the woodbox next to the stove where I went to keep warm, muttering to myself, 'You vile woman, you dreadful woman, you horrible, horrible woman.' "

Teddy glanced around the room. No one looked at March.

"To be fair," March said, "the childhood was not all

entirely bad. At one point when I was seven and Margaret three, Mother simply packed us up and dumped us with our paternal grandmother, Yuksa, on the reserve up the coast while Mother went back east to try her fortune alone.

"This period, I consider the only happy part of my childhood, the only time when I truly lived in grace. Were it not for dear, dear Yuksa, I'd be a raving loon. But two years later, Mother showed up with a ridiculous sapphire ring and," March heaved a great sigh, "*dragged* us back to Toronto to live with our new stepfather. It was a terrible time, terrible, one of the worst in my life. Because Yuksa couldn't write, I survived Toronto only by exchanging snippets of knitting with her, back and forth across the continent: mittens I could not thumb, hats too large for my head: Yuksa would carefully unravel them and make them good as new."

Gently Teddy asked, "And how is all this related to the map?"

"I'm coming to that." March glanced over to where the dolls sat on the counter. "You see, our dolls were given to us by one of mother's beaus in Victoria—did I tell you when they visited we were banished to the bedroom? So at Yuksa's the dollies were one of the few playthings we had. Yuksa made wonderful clothes for them, wonderful. Where she learned I'll never know."

"And the map?"

"Yes, yes. As I told you, before our generation, knowledge of the *Boston* had always been passed down aurally, but as far as we can tell, right before Mother came to cart us off to Toronto, Yuksa drew the map and sewed it in the lining of the valise. We carried that map all over Upper Canada, never even knowing. As it turned out, Yuksa trusted neither of our parents—Father was drinking heavily by then—and wouldn't tell either where the *Boston* lay, although Father gave her much grief over it. It was a source of great conflict.

"It wasn't until we had been in Toronto several years that Yuksa told my father that she had decided to skip a generation and that we possessed the map. Our very bitter father told this to the woman who was nursing him when he died. She, in turn, passed the information on to Margaret, who was teaching at U.B.C. at the time. Margaret was in possession of the dolls—she was the younger and had played with them longer than I—so Margaret decided that the dolls, and by extension the map, were hers. No amount of persuasion could make her see that it all belonged to us both. So there it stands: my sister is dead, the map is mine, anything we find on the bottom of Santa Gertrudis Cove belongs to me."

Tabor's eyes misted. "She really didn't deserve it, March. She was an incredible woman. I wish you—" She broke off.

Steamboat reached over to brush a bulky hand across Tabor's knee. "This is hard on you, isn't it, Cutie? You really liked Margaret Zimmerman."

Tabor stood, blinking back tears. "How about loved her?"

"Aw, Cutie." Steamboat rose too, and circled Tabor with his hammy arms. "Why not, when we get back, we move your stuff up to Vancouver so I can look after you?"

"Steamboat," Tabor unlocked his grip with her forearms, "the day you need to look after me is the day I start naming my teeth."

Steamboat's pink cheeks trembled. "But, Cutie, you don't understand. March is right. There's a lot about Margaret Zimmerman you don't know."

March rocked back and forth. "I knew it. I knew it."

"Knew what?" asked Tabor.

March cackled and beamed. "Your name's *Jasper* Stevens, isn't it, Cookie?"

A beeper sounded and Aurie reached for the pager on his belt. "Oops, that's me."

Teddy looked up, eyeing him keenly, trying to read from his face whether he had set the beeper off himself. Gratified, she watched as he snatched his phone from his duffel and went outside. "He's probably going to have to leave."

"Well, Cookie," resumed March. "Exactly when did you realize you were in the den of the enemy?"

"She wasn't the enemy. Besides, Tabor's here."

"What?" asked Tabor.

March forced a smile and hummed, dangling her foot happily. "Never mind. Never mind. Whenever you're ready. I still need to know if I can count on you lads tomorrow morning." She pinned Christian with her inky gaze. "What do you say, Boy? You heard my offer of halfsies, didn't you?"

"I don't mind going down, March. As long as we get back in time for the late ferry."

"But of course. You want me to show you the metal detector so you know what's what tomorrow? It's not a very new one, but I know it works."

Christian shrugged. "I've used them before."

Aurie swept back inside, combing his hair with his fingers. "Pretty bad crackup on I-5, they're asking for all the bone men to come in."

"Do you have to go right now?" asked Tabor.

Teddy watched his face for a lie, thoroughly enjoying the turn of events.

"Wouldn't hurt." Aurie turned to March. "How possible is it to get back to Gold River tonight?"

"I can lead you back," said March. "I suppose you're taking that fancy boat of yours."

Aurie fished the boat keys from his pocket and dropped them on the table. "No. You guys keep it." He turned to Christian. "Can you run it back up to Gold River and trailer it for me? I'll have somebody from Charlie Tuna's pick it up next week."

"Sure. Thanks."

"Good, good." March bobbed her foot happily. "Get yourself packed, Beamish, and I'll run you back myself. Since you won't be here, maybe Girlie can go down in your suit tomorrow."

"Hey, cool!" said Tabor.

Distractedly they watched Aurie pack when suddenly there came the most astounding sound from outside on the dock. It was a lyric tenor echoing across the cove.

> "Stets soll nur dir, nur dir mein Lied ertönen!
> Gesungen laut sei jetzt dien Preis von mir."

"It's Steamboat!" cried Teddy. They all held their breath to listen. Steamboat's voice rose sublimely in the night, the yearning so sweet it caught them by the throat and silenced them with awe. It was as if Steamboat shouldered all the longing of the earth and was offering it up to the sky.

> "Dein süsser Reiz ist Quelle alles Schönen,
> und jedes holde Wunder stammt von dir.
> Doch hin muss ich zur Welt der Erden,
> bei dir kann ich nur Sklave werden."

"What's he singing?" asked Tabor.

"Wagner," croaked March. "He's just told the Love Goddess he has to return to the world of men; with her he can only be a slave."

They listened as he finished the aria, then sat quietly when he came back inside. Sheepishly Steamboat collected dishes and started cleaning up.

Finally Teddy said, "That was beautiful, Steamboat."

"Hope I didn't scare the fish. It was just so pretty out there."

"Where did you learn opera?" Tabor's voice wavered with awe.

"I was a voice student at university. They still call me during season when they need to pad the chorus."

March pressed. "You were a boy soprano, weren't you?"

"That's right."

"She taught you English at U.B.C., didn't she, Cookie?"

Steamboat flushed crimson. "Her name was Margaret *Hunt* back then, wasn't it? She's got your black eyes."

"And she stole it, eh, Cookie? She stole your story."

Tabor stood. "What story? What are you two talking about?"

March's eyes gleamed wet with pleasure. "Wake up, Girlie, wake up. I want you to meet Yukon Boy."

12

Tabor dropped onto a chair. "I don't get it."

"Please don't think less of Margaret," said Steamboat.

"I don't."

March squinted keenly, relishing the scene. "Don't you see? Margaret stole his story when she taught him English. Cookie told her about singing to the wolves—how they saved his life when he slept in their den."

Steamboat bent to the sink, his reflection in the window wearing red chagrin. "I was trying to turn it into a book. I thought she might be able to help."

Christian panted, "What happened to you?"

Steamboat shrugged. "We were up fishing at Lake Laberge when I was eleven, it was early May. My dad and I'd been casting for trout, working our way upstream, and I got tired, so Dad gave me the fish and sent me back to camp. Some way or other I got my directions swapped—I thought all the streams flowed the same way—and I got messed up. So I kept on walking, and got really lost, and it got dark, so I started hanging up fish as markers. It kept getting colder and colder and then this wet snow starts falling—really big, sticky flakes. I didn't have any matches so I climbed under a fallen tree and tried to use branches to keep warm. Except everything was soaking wet.

"By that time it was totally dark, and the whole time I'd

132

been making a nest for myself, I felt somebody watching me, so I'd look up, not see anybody, then go back to making my nest. Then I yelled and yelled, but nobody came.

"Finally the moon comes out and I was freezing to death. The snow had stopped, and I see this white steam at the other end of the log, like somebody was down there. So I went over, and all of a sudden this mother wolf is right there staring me in the eye. I mean right there. Turns out, I'm in front of her den, with her puppies, just about to stick my hand in it."

"Wow."

"Yeah. So I go dead-still, I mean, I don't even breathe. The whole time, this mother wolf's watching me: these big silver eyes, waiting to see what I would do.

"So I just start talking to her: 'Nice wolfie, I won't hurt your babies.' But I was so cold I could feel the heat coming out of the den, and I wasn't about to go away, I didn't care if she killed me or not. So there I was: and I didn't move, and she didn't move, and all that worked was for me to keep on talking, so finally I started singing choir songs. After a while she sees I'm not leaving, and she comes up and starts digging at the mouth of the den, like it was okay, she was making it bigger for me. And then she nudges my hand, like I should dig too. Then finally the cubs stick their heads out. They were really cute." He held his hands a foot apart. "About this long. I climbed in in front of them, pulled up some branches, and fell asleep."

"When'd they find you?"

"I don't remember, middle of the night. They'd gone back to get some dogs. My dad said when they found me, the dogs didn't bark or anything. It was like, total respect. They knew she'd saved my life."

Tabor asked, "But what about in the book, when all the other wolves on the hillside sang with you?"

Steamboat shook his head. "Margaret made that part up."

"So you didn't really sing 'Panis Angelicus'?"

"Oh, sure. But I sang a lot of other stuff too. Benjamin Britten, German *lieder*, anything I could think of."

March grinned. "She gnarled your story so gnarly you didn't even recognize yourself, eh, Cookie?"

"She made it more exciting, if that's what you mean."

"So one day, after you'd long forgotten, you saw *Yukon Boy* in the bookstore. Opened it up and realized you'd been had, terribly had . . ."

March grabbed her boat keys on their yellow foam bobber. "See, Girlie. Lived in her own Cloud Cuckooland, to keep the world at bay." Jingling her keys, March looked at Aurie. "Come on, Beamish, let's go. I don't like being out at tide change."

Aurie picked up his duffel. "Well, folks, you've been interesting company. Guess I'll have to pick up a copy of *Yukon Boy* when I get back." He glanced wistfully at Teddy, who looked away. "Goodbye, everybody, good luck tomorrow."

"Thanks, Aurie. We'll take care of the skiff."

They listened to March's runabout speed off in the night and finally Tabor blurted, "Steamboat, you know how you said you always use the border crossing at Lynden?"

"Saves time."

"You didn't slip across before us the other night . . ."

"Cutie, no!" Steamboat rushed over, kneeling before her. "You've got to believe me. I didn't kill Margaret Zimmerman, I haven't thought about her in years."

"You swear?"

"Oh, Cutie. You don't know how much that hurts."

Tabor sighed. "I'm sorry." She walked to the corner and unfolded a flat air mattress. "But neither of her other books has a clue either. At least I can't find one."

Steamboat twisted a dishrag. "Please let me help you through this. I don't want anything to happen to you." Tormented, he looked away. "I just want to help."

"Steamboat, I've got to tell you something." Tabor glanced at Teddy, then faced Steamboat squarely. "I really appreciate your interest, but you need to know I'm gay. I'm just not interested, okay?"

Steamboat nodded. "I know. You told me that the first time."

"And if you keep this up, you're just going to get hurt."

"Naw, it's okay. I got it." He shook his head. "A lot of people love me, always have." He rubbed his forehead. "It's just—I still think you're one of the most amazing human beings I've ever met. I *really* like your style."

"My what?" Tabor colored. "Thank you. I didn't know I had any."

"Are you kidding? You got great style!"

Tabor bit her lip. "Thank you. But could you please not tell anybody else about this? If the breeder girls find out, they won't want to wrestle me."

"But Perfec—?" Steamboat's face looked like a Chinese puzzle. "Wait a minute, you mean you don't know about Perfecta?"

"What about her?"

"She's a lesbian. I mean, that's why I thought you were kidding me at first. I thought you got it from her. I mean, got the idea from her."

"Perfecta's gay?"

"Yeah, you gotta to meet her partner, she's one of the biggest women bankers in the city. They raise exotic animals over in North Vancouver. Have this great house."

Tabor stared.

"Libby Somebody, Hong Kong Bank. Talk to her if you ever need bankrolling for anything."

"Thank you, I will." Flustered at being the center of attention, Tabor picked up her air mattress and huffed into it.

Teddy went to the sink and dried dishes for Steamboat

while Christian scrutinized the diving tables from a paper-back.

''Where does everyone want to bunk tonight?'' Tabor asked.

''Is that 'bunk' as in 'floor'?'' asked Teddy.

A phone rang and Christian reached into his duffel, ex-asperated. ''I guess the dock is where we're taking our business calls tonight.'' He pulled up the antenna and walked out into the dark.

Tabor resumed, ''How about girls sleep in the kitchen and guys out in the store? Or other way around is fine, too.''

Teddy lowered her head in disappointment. In a few minutes Christian came back in and tossed his phone into his duffel. ''That was Angela again. I've got to go first thing in the morning.''

Teddy jerked her head. ''Why?''

''Now she can't find a whole set of Rosenthal china, as well as a silver tea set and a bunch of other stuff. When she asked Mrs. Dykstra about it, World's Favorite Nurse got huffy and walked out.''

''But why do you have to get involved?''

''Because Angela's last name is Lloyd and I'm the hired help.''

Teddy wiped a crackled blue dish. ''March isn't going to like this.''

''I know, but I've got to go.'' Christian addressed Steam-boat's broad backside at the sink. ''Steamboat, you can dive tomorrow, can't you?''

''Suit won't fit.''

''Then, Tabor, you and Teddy are going to have to do it yourselves.''

''Just the two of us? March is going to blow her stack.''

Christian exhaled deeply. ''I know. I know. We'll have to outflank her. I'll plot the dive and show you exactly what to do. Then when she comes in, we'll just tell her that it's all arranged. Teddy, did you watch us use the airbags today?''

''No. I was already topside.''

''In that case,'' Christian got up and took an orange rubber float from the pile of gear against the wall, ''you need to come look at this.''

Teddy dried her hands and knelt close beside him, waiting. The cool smell of outside still clung to his plaid. ''Well?''

''Well,'' he said. ''For starters, every time you descend thirty-three feet you double the pressure.''

Teddy gazed at him earnestly. ''That's interesting.''

''Not interesting, important. What it means is that if you fill this bag *full* of air down on the bottom, by the time it gets to the surface, it will be ready to explode, get it? It'll have double the air it can handle. What's more, if it's too full, when it reaches about fifteen feet, it'll start zipping up so fast, you won't be able to control it. So you really don't want to overfill it.''

''I popped to the surface too fast myself today. My nose was bleeding.''

He frowned. ''Listen, you guys've got to do this right.''

''So what do I do?''

''What you do is pay attention to neutral gravity. Only pipe in enough air to get your salvage hanging there in the water, then you and Tabor start pulling the whole thing up yourselves. By the time you get to the surface, the airbag's going to be entirely full of air.''

He regarded her mildly. ''And as for your nose, don't have your vest too full when you're ready to surface—or more importantly—your lungs.''

''*That*, I remember: 'Breathe normally all the way up.' ''

''Good.'' He stood and plucked a pencil from an antique tea tin on the sill. Sketching a long ovoid on the flyleaf of his book, he filled in a line of blackened ''o's'' to represent the exposed ribs of the *Boston*, then sketched a black square near the bow.

"Is that square supposed to be the forge?" asked Tabor.

"No, that's the cookstove we found today. I wish I had a better sense of what was actually down there."

"Tabor," said Teddy. "Where did March put that journal?"

Tabor climbed halfway up the dark stairs and fumbled through the bookcase. Holding up the green volume, she said, "It's not really a journal. It's a book published . . ." She leafed pages. ". . . in 1896 in London." She read, " 'The Adventures and Suffering of John R. Jewitt only survivor of the crew of the ship *Boston* during a captivity of nearly three years among the Indians of Nootka Sound in Vancouver Island.' "

She handed it to Christian, who leafed the thick ivory pages. "Where's the part about the shipwreck?" he asked.

"Who knows." Tabor resumed work on her air mattress.

Teddy peeked over his shoulder. "Check for a table of contents. Or an index."

Christian searched the front of the book, then the back, with no luck.

"Then you'll just have to follow his trip chronologically."

Christian handed the book to her. "Yours, Morelli. Go to it."

Teddy sat down at the table and ran her fingers over the gleaming filigree on the cover. Inside, the swollen Bodoni typeface was fat as the cheeks of cherubs. She turned the deckle-edged pages and thought of the thick Florentine art paper that students swooned over in the bookstore. Browsing a moment, she said, "Hey, listen to this. 'I was sent for by my neighbor Yealthlower to file his teeth, which operation having performed, he informed me that his new wife, whom he had a little time before purchased, having refused to sleep with him, it was his intention to bite off her nose. I endeavored to dissuade him, but he was determined, and in fact, performed his savage threat that very night, saying that since she would not be his wife, she should not be that of any other, and in the morning sent her back to her father.' ''

Ignoring her, Christian asked, "Does anybody know where March keeps the metal detector? I should show you guys how to use it."

Steamboat stirred. "In the shed. I'll get it."

"Ugh!" said Teddy. "You've got to hear this."

"Come on, Teddy." Tabor plugged her mattress. "Get on the program."

"No, listen. This is great: 'At their meals they made a practice of taking vermin from their heads or clothes and eating them, by turns thrusting their fingers into their hair, and into the dish, and spreading their garments over the tubs in which the provision was cooking, in order to set in motion their inhabitants.' Isn't that wonderful?"

"You're racist for reading that."

"No, you don't get it. There's all kinds of equally repulsive things that Europeans do that we just take for granted."

"No, we don't. Like what?"

"Can you imagine what it looks like the first time you watch someone blow their nasal mucus into a little white cloth, then put it back in their pocket?"

"Come on, Teddy, we don't have all night."

Teddy flipped to the front of the book. "Most of this is about Jewitt's captivity, so I'm guessing the details of the ship are in the front." She skimmed quickly. "Okay, here he is in Hull, England."

'' '. . . the ship having undergone a thorough repair and been well coppered, proceeded to take on board her cargo, which consisted of English cloths, Dutch blankets.' Hmm . . . Okay, here we go. 'I found myself well accommodated on board as regarded my work, an iron forge having been erected on deck; this my father had made for the ship on a new plan, for which he afterwards obtained a patent; while a corner of the steerage was appropriated to my vise bench so that in bad weather I could work below.' ''

''That's what March read last time,'' said Tabor.

''Great,'' said Christian. ''What else?''

''That's it. Next thing is they're sailing past the Brazils and Cape Horn.''

''... a corner of steerage,'' Christian murmured. He drew a second square midstern. ''Okay, the vise bench is going to be back here someplace. So when you use the metal detector and it buzzes near the stern, don't start digging there, got it?''

Teddy read again. '' ' ... in a *corner* of the steerage appropriated to my vise bench.' ''

''Okay, we'll put it in a corner.'' Christian erased his square and drew two dashed-lined boxes at either corner of the stern. ''Your vise bench is in either of these two corners so don't dig for it. Now tell me again about the forge.''

'' ' ... an iron forge having been erected on deck.' That's it.''

''Swell. 'Erected on deck.' I tend to think they'd put a forge forward, as a counterbalance for the cookstove.'' He drew a square on the port side forward, exactly across from the stove. ''That'd be my first guess.''

''Christian, why was the cookstove out on deck like that today? It seems a dumb place to cook,'' said Tabor.

''I'm pretty sure stoves were on the second deck down and had a vent up to the outside. Probably the deck above rotted away.''

''Then why isn't our forge sitting out too?''

''Good question, it might be. I guess I just thought Aurie had it all wrapped up for us, I didn't even try to look through all that silt.'' Christian worked busily at his diagram, plotting estimated distances, and finally making Tabor and Teddy memorize it.

"It's pretty straightforward," he said. "The only thing is, if you need the metal detector, you're going to have to learn how to distinguish between big things, like the forge, and all the little stuff you're going to find: metal fittings, nails." He set the earphones of the metal detector on Teddy's head and handed her the weedeater-style wand.

"Okay, these are your controls: off-on, volume, discriminator."

"Discriminator," she repeated. "What's this other one?"

"Battery test, don't worry about it."

She flipped the "on" switch and listened to the faint buzzing sound as she passed the wand across the floor. "Do I set the discriminator on 'high' to filter out the little stuff?"

"That's right, good."

She turned up the discriminator and the buzzing disappeared. Waving the wand in front of the woodstove, the earphones buzzed like angry hornets. "Okay, I can do this."

"I want to try," said Tabor.

Teddy played with the controls a bit and pulled off the earphones to find everyone frozen in place, rigid with listening. Through the floorboards she felt the rich prickly sound of a boat far out on the channel.

"She's coming," whispered Tabor.

"It's okay." Steamboat's voice was a balm. "We're ready for her."

They listened to March tie up, muttering and cackling to herself. They heard her stop to use the outhouse then, seconds later, burst through the kitchen door. Stopping suddenly, she read their faces. "What's going on here?"

Christian offered his drawing. "March, I got a phone call and I have to go first thing in the morning. I've plotted the dive out for Teddy and Tabor, everything's under control. They'll take care of it just fine.''

''What's that you say?'' she shouted.

His chest heaved. ''I said I have to leave. The women will dive for you.''

March's face blurred like melting wax. ''No, Boy. You're wrong. You *don't* have to go. You have to help me pull up my forge.''

''March, it's out of my control. They need me back home.'' He gestured to Tabor. ''Tabor and Teddy have learned how to use the metal detector and airbags. Steamboat is going to help out from the boat.''

Steamboat soothed, ''We can do it, March.''

The guttural sound started as a low rumble in March's throat and turned into a roar. ''*Noooo!* You're not leaving. Do you hear me?'' Reeling across the room, she clutched the yellow bobber with her boat keys in her fist, opened the kitchen door and hurled the keys into the cove.

''March, stop!''

Next March snatched up Christian's and Aurie's keys from the table and balled them in a fist above her head. ''I don't care if we all die here! We're going after my gold.'' She cocked her arm to throw.

''March, wait!'' Christian blocked the door. ''Put the keys down. This isn't funny.''

''Funny?'' she bellowed. Clenching the keys to her temples, she staggered across the room. ''God in heaven, how do I stand it? Funny?'' She slumped into a chair next to the Monarch and rocked, hugging her arms. In the cold silence that followed, winter air swirled through the kitchen and Steamboat, with infinite calm, walked over and closed the door.

''You're going to put those ninnies down there in wetsuits?'' croaked March. ''Why don't we just drown them both tonight in the cove?''

No one came to the sisters' defense.

For a minute no one spoke. Gradually all eyes focused on Christian, waiting. He said, "If I don't go home, I'll probably lose my job."

March persisted. "Who's to know how long it takes you to get home? Six hours, twelve hours? What's that woman going to do?"

Christian looked around at the hopeful eyes. Finally, he sighed. "Well, I guess I can stay, at least for one dive."

"Ha!" March bounced up, cackling. "Of course you can."

"But, March, I'm telling you, if we don't find the forge first thing in the morning, I'm leaving anyway. Got it?"

"We'll find it. We'll find it. Glad you have the girls all primed." Merrily, she dug into her sweater pocket and pulled out a folded note. "Oh, Freddy," she sang. "Beamish wrote you a letter on the way back to Gold River. I think he's in love with you."

Teddy frowned. "Thank you."

"A little full of himself, but he's a good heart."

Teddy casually tucked the letter under *Jewitt* to let everyone know that Aurie's feelings were of no importance to her.

Tabor stood. "We better get to bed, guys. We want to be in the water as soon as it's light."

"That's right." March poked inside the firebox and bounded up the stairs to the loft. "Also, I'm a light sleeper and I won't have any funnybugging in my house."

In astonished silence, they savored the word.

"Good night, March," said Steamboat.

They watched her disappear up the stairs and the two men took their gear to the front room.

"No funnybugging, guys," whispered Tabor.

"Shhh." They pulled the printed curtain closed behind them.

Next to the stove Teddy unrolled her backpacking mattress and sleeping bag, then stripped down to long underwear. Zipping herself into the bag, she unfolded Aurie's letter as Tabor fussed about with stuck zippers and wet socks. The letter was written in blotchy ballpoint on the title page of the Vancouver Island tide book. The sight of Aurie's cramped handwriting stirred sleeping parts of her soul. She read.

Dear Teddy,

I realize that you'll probably throw this into the stove as soon as you get it, but I had to give it a try. I know from your point of view, I deserve all the vituperation your adorable little body can muster.

"Eat dirt."
"What?" asked Tabor.
"Nothing."

But I also know that neither of us has fundamentally changed over the past six years, and for that I am profoundly thankful.

In spite of your justifiable anger the other night, I was astonished at how peaceful it feels to be with you again. After five years of playing clean-up for the Princess of Me, it feels like coming home. God, it was bliss. I had forgotten how fast an intelligent woman can move a conversation along, and how wonderful it is to be acknowledged when you speak. Even arguing with you was wonderful. Thank you, thank you, even if I never see you again. At least I know what I'm looking for.

Of course you're absolutely right: I deserved everything I got when I married a hood ornament. To be truthful, when I first met Jennifer and saw I had a chance, I honestly thought I could mutate into the sleek, urbane jetsetter worthy of so ornamental a

woman. *(We're walking a fine line here, you're awfully ornamental yourself.)* But, now, after tap-
dancing at high-speed for five years, I'm just plain
tired; I find I want a companion rather than a trophy,
a partner rather than a flaming charge card.

*(For some reason I feel like I'm writing a person-
als ad—SDPhys seeks ShtBrunHist for friendship and
???—so I think I'd better close.)*

I'd apologize again for not acknowledging your
translations in my Isthmus article, but we've been
through that enough, haven't we? Which reminds me:
a dermatologist down the hall translates Roman po-
ets. I've got some Lucretius pinned above my desk:

Oh, blind heart,
In what darkness of life, in what great dangers
ye spend this little span of years.

*On that happy note I'll close.
I remain your faithful admirer,*

Aurie

P.S. We've always known Mama's escritoire was
nineteenth century. On the bottom it says "Bienville,
Paris," an atelier that opened in 1854.
P.P.S. If what's-his-name had a stroke, I don't
think he would have bitten through his bottom lip.

Teddy held the letter for a full ten seconds, rehearsing
the moves necessary to toss it into the stove. Finally her
forearm quivered and she folded it and put it away.

"What's Aurie got to say?" Tabor climbed into her
sleeping bag.

"Typical Aurie stuff."

"Too bad. He's really a kick."

"I know. It is too bad."

Next morning Teddy slipped on clothes to tiptoe to the outhouse. On the dock she found March dipping into the glassy cove with a gaff hook. "Good morning, Freddy," she said sweetly.

Teddy walked over. March was retrieving a yellow floating object.

"What's that?" asked Teddy.

"Shhh." March freed the bauble from her gaff hook and held it up: the yellow foam bobber with her boat keys. Eyes glinting like a harbor seal's, March whispered, "I'll tell you a secret, Freddy, but you mustn't tell a soul: the tide sweeps this way at night."

Back inside, the others were stirring and March had them all fed and on the dock before they had time to comb their hair. After setting out the ski boat as Bailley's decoy again, Teddy, Christian, Tabor, and Steamboat huddled in the pilothouse of Aurie's sturdy skiff and followed March down the channel.

Wedged between the wall and the steering wheel, Teddy tugged at her wetsuit, trying to mold it to her body. "I really don't want to go down again."

Christian eyed her for signs of distress. "I don't think we have a choice."

"You certainly are being big about all this. If she had played that trick with the boat keys on me, I would have left immediately."

"I actually thought about it, but then I realized the woman's deranged and I shouldn't leave you all here alone."

Teddy smiled. "I'm sorry I got you into this. I should have put a stop to this before it started."

"Speaking of deranged." Tabor eyed Steamboat, who

nodded silent assent. "I guess we should tell you guys now."

"Tell us what?"

Reaching into a scuba duffel, Tabor pulled out a laminated aluminum hamburger wrapper. "Steamboat found this in March's boat yesterday and realized it couldn't possibly be from around here. Guess where it *is* from?"

It was familiar trash and Teddy smoothed it open against the console. " 'The Web Locker,' " she read. "That's in the marina in Bellingham!"

"Smell it. Means March was just there."

"You're right! So, when she said she talked to Margaret before she died, she was actually down in Bellingham."

Tabor nodded, saying each word individually. "Yes. Like-maybe-on-the-same-day-Margaret-was-killed?"

Christian looked away from his piloting. "You'd better save that, Tabor. It might be important."

"I know." Tabor folded the wrapper and queried Steamboat respectfully. "You want to keep it, or should I?"

"You, Babe." Steamboat's voice had a new warmth.

"Are we still going to dive for her?" asked Teddy.

Christian shrugged. "What else can we do? Tell her we won't dive because we think she killed her sister? How do we know she won't knock holes in the boats this time?"

"What if when we're in the water she . . ." Teddy didn't know how to finish.

Christian shook his head. "I don't think she can hurt anybody. Steamboat's going to be up here with her." He added, "It's not like she's in charge of our air or anything."

They anchored next to the craggy rocks with mussels in the clefts and scared away a family of seals. The dull sun was a cotton ball in gray fleece, and seagulls cried like babies without breakfast. Steamboat lashed the boats together while Tabor, Teddy, and Christian strapped on scuba equipment. After testing each other's valves and pipes and gauges, they lowered the airbags and metal detector and filled their vests for the dive. Crinkling in her trash bag, March was as irritable as wasps. "Why is this taking so long?"

"Three times the labor, three times the money," said Christian. "Ready, folks?" He sat on the gunnels to fall backwards. Then he splashed. Tabor sat down, then tilted backwards to join him. Next it was Teddy's turn. Gritting her teeth, she splashed.

"Yow!" she screamed. It was no better than the first time, maybe worse. White pain poured down her spine as the water once again found baggy spots in her suit.

Christian treaded beside her. "Ready?"

They pressed the release valves on their vests and slowly descended into the chartreuse haze. The icy ache on Teddy's exposed cheeks felt like the grip of a vise. Again she calmed herself with the sound of her own breathing: Darth Vader versus the Happy Bubbler. Touching down, she and Tabor finned over behind Christian to the already lowered metal detector and airbags, then watched as he untied the detector from a line and left a large rock to help weigh down the airbags.

Stumbling right into the row of black stubs, they found the depression where the cookstove had been. Christian put on the earphones to scan the sand directly across the keel from it. Finding nothing, he turned the discriminator lower and immediately hit a buzz. Motioning for Tabor and Teddy to dig with their hands, they quickly uncovered a crumbly black lump and a scabrous cleat. They dug further, and Christian put his hand on their arms and motioned "cut" across his neck. They stopped digging.

Next Christian swam with the metal detector to the stern of the boat. Teddy and Tabor followed and watched as he turned the discriminator back on high. Within seconds he lifted his head and motioned "thumbs up" and then waved them close to let them both listen to the port corner of steerage. "Vise bench." They all nodded to each other. Which was not what they needed at all.

Then Tabor excitedly grabbed their arms, wanting to pantomime an idea. Hands cupped like the hull of a ship, she lowered them slowly in front of her, tilting them to the side. Then, with a finger she showed a object sliding off the deck, landing far away from the side of the boat.

Christian nodded, liking the idea. He swam bow-ward again to the spot across from the cookstove, then turned outward and swam away from the ship. Sweeping the sand with the metal detector, he worked systematically back and forth through the limy haze, moving farther and farther away from the ship.

Unable to see more than ten yards in front of her, Teddy stayed close to the wooden stubs, waiting patiently until they could go up and tell March the forge wasn't there. She amused herself by touching sea cucumbers to watch them shrivel, then surprised a flounder—and herself—camouflaged in the sand. She watched as it swam off toward a large dark boulder, then realized that boulders should not be present on a sandy bottom. Finning over, she discovered a crumbly iron object about half the size of the cookstove. Eagerly she swam back to Christian and Tabor, waving them over with exaggerated motions.

Rushing back, they hovered in a circle as Christian broke off a piece like black pie crust. "Okay," he signaled, and swam over to retrieve the airbags. Teddy and Tabor began digging tunnels under the object, banging their foreheads as they finned to stay close. Christian came back and the three dug eagerly, Teddy remembering to keep calm so her air supply would last.

Finally the object was ready to be strapped in. Christian worked the bands of the airbags underneath from two directions and filled the orange bags slightly with air from his safe-second. They tugged a bit. Nothing happened. Pumping in more air, they watched as the black lump slowly heaved and righted. Christian added a squirt more of air, and the cargo floated free, hovering several inches off the bottom. He motioned "thumbs up" and they all proudly grabbed airbag straps for the trip to the surface.

In bubbly commotion they popped into the commonplace world.

"Did you find it?" bellowed March.

Christian ripped off his mask. "We found something."

They trawled the airbags over to the hoist, strapped in the black hulk, and watched as Steamboat worked the pulley and March steadied the cargo with her knobby hands. Climbing out of the water, they arrived just as Steamboat lowered the dripping black lump into the cockpit.

"How do we know it's the forge?" asked Steamboat.

"We don't." March waved impatiently for Christian's diving knife. "It could be Captain Cook's chamber pot for all we know. We'll have to break into it and see what's there."

Christian unsnapped the knife sheaf on his arm and whipped out the eight-inch blade. March dug into the black hunk. "This is too smooth. This isn't the bottom."

Christian looked at both ragged ends. "I vote for the ash drawer being on the side by the rail."

March grunted and leaned over, poking ineffectually in the cramped space. "I can't dig this way. You'll have to turn it around."

"I can get in there," said Teddy. She squeezed herself in the space between the bulkhead and the forge and put her hand out for the knife. March reluctantly handed it in and Teddy began jabbing the brittle iron, flinching as great chunks flew off into her face. "All this is, is dead cast iron."

"Keep digging."

"Take the whole thing apart if you have to, which reminds me, Freddy. I made a Chinook list for you, I tucked it in the bag."

"Thank you." The soft iron was the consistency of stale pound cake. Each jab of the knife broke off chunks of metal salts that clattered to the deck, leaving edges sharp enough to pierce the neoprene suits. Suddenly one jab of the knife cleaved off a platelike slab, its pearl-gray face clearly a different element. "Hey, this is ashes."

She jabbed again and a pale chunk the size of a football fell in her lap. She picked it up and turned it over. "Wait a minute! There's something in here." Brushing away bits of gray fry with her fingers, she found a smooth yellow coin inside. There was a coat of arms with an Irish harp in the corner. Clawing away crumbs, she touched raised numbers circling the top. "17—" She scratched some more. "—67. It's gold! This whole *thing* is gold."

They whooped like cowboys, then listened gleefully as their echoes shouted from the shore.

Teddy pried loose the coin and held it up. On the obverse the unmistakably double-chinned George III wore a laurel wreath and stared off into time. "Georgius III, Dei Gratia," she read.

They whooped again.

Handing the coin to March, she stood up to ease her back.

"Don't stop, Freddy, there's more in there. Toss me that first chunk. I'll dig the coins out of it while you look for more."

Across the gunnels they passed the heavy chunk of gold-laced ash to March, and Teddy resumed her position. Chinking away with the knife, she said, "Actually, March, I think it all came off at once. But I'll keep looking."

"Of course you will. It's there."

Teddy stopped to wrap the knife handle in her wetsuit bonnet so it wouldn't cause blisters.

Steamboat asked, "Want me to turn the forge around, Teddy? We might be able to help."

"I'm doing okay. I just don't think there's anything else in here. March."

March didn't answer.

"You need anything, Teddy?" asked Tabor.

"Doing fine," she called. "March, I really don't think there's anything else in here. March?"

Suddenly an engine revved.

"March!"

They looked up to see March zipping across the cove in her ramshackle boat.

"She's taking the gold!"

"Catch her!"

Christian squinted at the retreating boat. "That was dumb. We can beat her home."

Steamboat smiled, vastly amused. "She isn't going *home*. She'll go hole up in a cove somewhere. She knows we can't stay."

Tabor's voice broke. "But she hasn't told me about Margaret. She promised!"

A shocking horn brayed. "*Toooot*." The sound vibrated through their bones while down at the mouth of the cove a huge handsome blue-hulled vessel came into view. She was flying the Maple Leaf and her wheelhouse brandished an elegantly gilded crest.

"Coast Guard," cried Tabor.

"Mounties," corrected Steamboat.

Behind the vessel chugged Mr. Bailley's posh lavender troller looking like the Little Boat who had brought his big brother to the fray. In his gleaming masts spun more electronic whirligigs than the government boat.

Everyone gawked as the two boats headed toward March's bow, mounties in orange cruiser suits attentive on deck. March swerved twice, changing course, then realized she was outpowered and outfinessed. Cutting her engine, she dashed out of her rickety cabin and screamed at the smoke-tinted windows of the lavender wheelhouse. "Bailley!" Her voice echoed across the cove. "I'll get you!"

13

"Quick, everybody. Other side of the boat." Steamboat herded them all to port. Squatting into a deep knee bend, he lifted the black forge, his back erect. "Everybody ready?"

"Ready." They held on.

With an enormous grunt, Steamboat hoisted the forge and pitched it over the gunnels. It disappeared in a splash, while the boat rocked back and forth, trying to right itself.

"Do you think they saw?" asked Tabor.

"Doesn't matter." Steamboat watched it sink. "Possession is the issue."

"What are we going to say?"

"Not *one* word, unless you're spoken to." Steamboat looked around. "Christian, do you think you can you handle this? Maybe they'll think we're all American." He meant "stupid."

"Sure." Christian pulled off his hood. "Guess we better haul up the metal detector."

They reeled up the detector as they watched the little drama unfold across the cove: an orange-clad mountie boarding March's tiny vessel and handing up the lumpy black boulder to an officer in a navy baseball cap. He, in turn, handed it to his commanding officer, who leaned over the rail and held his polite demeanor with the contentious March. Finally she climbed the rope ladder to the cutter's deck and clumped back to the stern in her heavy boots. Shaking a fist in the air, she once more hurled invectives at Bailley's tinted windows. Then the mounties tied her runabout to their stern and began towing it toward Aurie's skiff.

"What's Mr. Bailley got to do with this anyway?" asked Teddy.

Steamboat sloshed water over the deck to send iron flakes into the scuttles. "I would imagine the local Indian band is pretty touchy about who dives for what around here, and it doesn't look like too much gets by Mr. Bailley. Look virtuous, here they come."

Casual as hell, Christian reached under the console and pulled out Aurie's M&Ms. "Candy, anybody?"

They held out their hands and Steamboat said, "Did you know you can use the blue ones to dye eggs?"

"That right?"

"Don't say?"

They crunched candy, faces as innocent as milk.

The mounties drew up alongside, stopping directly over the wreck. Christian called cheerily to a man on the bow, "Good morning, officer."

The mountie eyed the fluttering stars-and-stripes off the stern. "Good morning, sir. Where'd you clear inward?"

"Towed over at Blaine yesterday."

"Been diving in the area?"

Christian shrugged. "Been helping a friend."

"Very good, sir. The problem is that your friend doesn't have papers from the Department of Transport to prove legal ownership of any wrecks in the area."

"Really? We had no idea."

The mountie exchanged glances with a comrade and looked back at Christian. "Yes, sir. We thought that might be the case." He wedged his clipboard against his chest and wrote. There was an awkward silence.

Finally Christian asked, "What should we do now?"

The mountie looked up. "Enjoy your stay, sir." He signaled to the pilothouse and the cutter started up. They all exhaled in relief and in the fresh biting silence, life suddenly drained from the group. Instead of a band of treasure seekers, they were simply four cold people in a miserable place on a equally miserable day.

Christian reached for the ignition. "You guys ready to go home?"

Their quiet was assent.

They puttered back to Morgan Cove and as March's cabin came into view, Teddy asked, "How are we going to get our stuff?"

Christian glanced at her. "How good are you at climbing?"

"Oh, dear."

"She leaves her attic window open."

Teddy turned to Steamboat. "Is it called 'breaking and entering' in Canada?"

Steamboat pulled his hat down over his eyes.

They docked at the raft and Steamboat clambered out to brace himself against the shingled cottage. Teddy, climbing cheerleader-style, stepped on his thigh, his shoulder, then scrambled up the roof. Slipping in the open window, she tumbled onto March's Japanese futon and bounded down the stairs to open the door for the others. They packed their gear quickly, waiting while Christian motored down the cove to retrieve his ski boat.

When Christian came back, he asked, "Steamboat, can you drive Aurie's skiff to Gold River?"

"Sure. As long as you let me have my chart."

Reluctantly, Christian handed over Canadian Hydrographic Chart #3664. "Then we'll have to follow you. There's some real muck out there in Hanna Channel."

"Wait, Steamboat." Cheerily Tabor rummaged in her duffel. "I'll go back with you. We can use my chart."

Steamboat glowed as if his wick were turned up.

The skiff and the ski boat motored in tandem into the great watery heart of Vancouver Island. Back at Gold River, they docked the boats one by one and pulled their trailers up to the pulp mill fence. Christian took out his cell phone and walked away. "I better tell Angela I'm coming."

"Fine," said Teddy. "I'll hurry Tabor along so we can get moving."

She walked down to Steamboat's pickup to find her sister serenely reading a road map in the front seat. Steamboat stepped up to meet Teddy, his face flushed with pleasure. "Tabor's coming with me. First we're going to haul Aurie's boat to Bellingham, then she's going to pick up her gear at your house."

"Her gear? Where's she going?"

Steamboat blushed. "She's moving into my place for a while, until we can find her an apartment in Vancouver."

"Fine." Teddy tried to control her face. "Steamboat, you do know not to expect too much, don't you? I mean, I don't want your feelings . . ."

"Listen." Steamboat shook his head. "We're gonna make her a star. You just watch."

"Well, good luck."

"Sure you don't want to come, too? Like I said, it'd be that much easier with the two of you."

"Gee, Steamboat, *nice* offer, but I think I'd better pass. Could you just make sure Tabor takes her barbell when she goes?"

"You bet." Steamboat extended his mammoth hand and Teddy took it eagerly, knowing how tender it would be. "Thanks for everything, Steamboat. You're a prince."

"My pleasure."

She watched his blue truck climb the valley, towing the looming silver hull, then she joined Christian in his Jeep. She stretched luxuriously. "Home sweet home," she muttered. "Hot water and soft beds."

Christian put away the phone, frowning.

"What's the matter?"

"We have an errand to do on the way south. Angela wants me to stop by Nurse Dykstra's and see if she's got the china."

"She stole it?"

"Don't know yet."

"But why do you have to do that?"

"I'm what's called middle management, which is another name for 'lackey-to-the-rich.'"

"Mrs. Dykstra lives out by Margaret. Next door, I think."

"You're kidding?" Christian dropped his keys.

"Is something the matter?"

"Well, I don't know yet."

Exhausted, they drove four hours down-island in silence, dozed on the ferry, and crossed the border at Lynden to avoid the long lines at the Peace Arch. At the Nooksack River bridge, Christian turned left, following the route Teddy and Tabor had taken Wednesday night. They whizzed by Margaret's red rural mailbox welded to the half-buried tractor tire. "There," said Teddy.

"Interesting."

They drove another hundred yards and Christian turned into a dirt drive. Jouncing down the road, Teddy caught a quick glimpse of a well-traveled path beat through the woods towards Margaret's. Her heart thumped in her chest. "How are you going to ask her about the china, Christian?"

"Beats me. Got any ideas?"

At the end of the drive they came to a pale green farmhouse with duck cutouts nailed to the window sash. They climbed from the Jeep and Mrs. Dykstra burst onto the front porch, arms crossed against the cold. By way of greeting, she said, "You two."

"Hello, Mrs. Dykstra."

"What can I do for you?" She looked back and forth between them, then settled on Christian.

"Mrs. Dykstra, we were on the way down from Canada and thought we'd stop by. May we come in?"

She stepped in front of the door. "I'd rather you didn't. My grandbaby's sleeping right now."

Christian stamped and shivered, accepting the limits of the porch. "Okay, then, real quick: Angela got a call from the funeral home, they said Mr. Lloyd's nose was broken. You know anything about it? They want Angela to sign a waiver."

"Sorry, I'm not involved anymore. You *do* know I quit work, don't you?"

"Yes, I heard." Christian shrugged. "I guess if the job's done, there's no point in staying."

"That's right." The nurse relaxed. "My agency is going to reassign me as soon as I'm ready." She huffed white breath. "Can I go now?"

"Ahh."

"Mrs. Dykstra," Teddy stumbled forward. "The reason we were in B.C. was to visit Margaret Zimmerman's older sister. She said Margaret was writing a story about the Nooksack River flood with the neighbor lady. That wouldn't be you, would it?"

"Her sister? You don't say." Shivering, the nurse stepped inside, allowing her guests entry onto the interior rattan mat. "Is this the same sister who scuttled their mother's houseboat when she was twelve?"

Christian whistled. "She didn't tell us that."

In the next room a T.V. blared and a large man leaned forward in his recliner to peek around the corner. Over the T.V. hung a gun rack laden with rural firearms. Christian smiled and took two steps forward. "Hi, Mr. Dykstra, who's winning?"

"Flea-hawks right now. Don't worry, they'll blow it."

Mrs. Dykstra quickly positioned herself in front of Christian so he could not enter any farther.

Mr. Dykstra asked, "Need anything, baby?"

"No, Ray. I'm fine."

Mr. Dykstra closed the T.V. room door and Mrs. Dykstra turned back to her guests, curling her lip. "This sister isn't going to try to write the flood story herself, is she?"

"I don't think so."

"Good." Mrs. Dykstra shook her head. "I thought the whole thing was just rubbish."

"Why?"

Venomously, Dykstra lashed, "That woman no more cared about the real flood than my pet rock. I told her I found a dead possum in my bedroom, she wrote it was a dead horse. I told her the men moved boulders onto the graveplots to keep the bodies down, she had coffins swirling around the cottonwood trees. I just about fell off my chair. I mean, besides being a lie, that's no story for children."

"You don't happen to have a copy, do you?"

The nurse recoiled. "Not me. Margaret gave me a rough draft and I wrote all over it, told her what I thought." She folded her arms once more. "Is that all, Christian? I should go check on my granddaughter."

"Ah, no." Christian searched the room. "I know you're not affiliated with the family any more, but I wondered if you had any professional assessment of why Mr. Lloyd's nose was broken?"

"I wouldn't worry about it. They drop them all the time at the funeral home."

"Interesting. Then why do you suppose they're making such a big deal out of it this time?"

"Lawsuits. They always make a fuss when money's involved."

"Ahh, you didn't happen to hear about any inventory being missing from the house, did you?"

"No." Mrs. Dykstra tucked her hands into her apron pockets. "I worked upstairs. I don't know anything about that."

"I'm surprised." Christian mumbled. "I—um . . ."

"What?" demanded Dykstra. Casually she walked to the door.

In her pocket Teddy fingered two saved M&Ms—blue ones, to try on eggs. "Mrs. Dykstra." She dug out the M&Ms and jiggled them in her fist. "I have a terrible headache, do you mind if I get some water?"

Swiftly Christian moved aside, standing between Mrs. Dykstra and the kitchen. As Teddy swept past, he continued, "Well, back to Mr. Lloyd's nose, if somebody mentions the idea of foul play, do you think there was the possibility of that?"

"Don't be silly." Mrs. Dykstra glanced at Teddy in the kitchen, then stepped back to block Christian, who tried to join her. "The man died of a stroke. And nobody could have gotten into that house. Have you ever heard the alarm in that place?"

In the kitchen Teddy turned on the water and examined the cupboards, trying to figure out which one would house a set of pilfered china. Eliminating the cabinet over the dishwasher as one for the everyday dishes, she opted for the cupboard closest to the dining room. She opened it gently, and spied a tall stack of ivory plates trimmed in cobalt and gold. Next to the plates were matching bread dishes, coffee cups, and fluted two-handled bouillon bowls. The shelf above held gold-trimmed chocolate pots, lidded serving dishes, and tiny elegant sugar and creamers. Quickly she closed the cabinet and swallowed the M&Ms, gulping water at the sink from her hand.

Mrs. Dykstra poked her head through the doorway. "Glasses are above the dishwasher."

Teddy waved her away. "I'm fine, thank you." She feigned head pain and flashed triumph at Christian.

"Well, Mrs. Dykstra." Christian extended his hand. "I guess we won't bother you anymore. Won't be the same without you over there at the house."

Mrs. Dykstra warily put out her hand. "Won't be the same for anyone anymore. They going to keep you?"

"Are you kidding?" Christian laughed. "I'm the only one dumb enough to do all their grunt work for them."

"Yes. Well, goodbye."

"Goodbye."

Out in the jeep, Christian started the engine and twisted around to back up. "Well?"

"There's china all right. Lots. Like maybe sixteen place settings, blue and gold trim."

"That's it."

"What are you going to do?"

"Tell Angela for starters." He drove a few moments in silence, then said, "Thank you for doing that."

"You're entirely welcome. I wanted to get out of there as badly as you."

They drove home cozily in the late afternoon haze, compatriots in crime. Pulling into Teddy's cul-de-sac, they found Aurie's aluminum boat looming in the drive.

"They beat us. I wonder where they are?" Teddy peeked into the garage. "Tabor's car's still there."

"Then they'll be back."

"I know. She doesn't have a house key."

Silently they unloaded gear onto Teddy's front porch.

"Well, Christian." Intrepidly she lifted her chin to be kissed. "It was an interesting weekend. Thank you for asking me."

Hesitating a full second, Christian swiftly brushed his lips across hers. Then he dashed to his Jeep.

Confused and disappointed, Teddy watched him drive away. She had never been insulted by a kiss before.

Unlocking her door, she padded back to the living room,

arms full of gear. Abruptly she stopped, dropping her things. ''No!'' she howled.

All the bookcases had been emptied onto the floor. The whole room was a shambles.

14

Stone-still, she listened. There was no sound.

Teddy picked her way over to the sliding glass door. The aluminum safety pole was bent L-shaped. The sturdy metal latch hook was hanging from the frame. Someone had pried open the door with a stiff bar, and—from the looks of it—had barely suffered a moment's delay.

"Damn." Scanning the room, she found the telephone unplugged on the dining table, neatly stacked on top of her clock radio and a huge picture book of French chateaux. Evidently the thief had had some second thoughts.

She jacked in the phone and immediately the message light came on; it had actually saved a call after being unplugged. Ignoring the light, she punched 911 and looked around. Her VCR was gone, as was the entire rack of CDs and tapes. They had taken her whole sound system except— she laughed nervously—her tinny grad school speakers.

"Emergency Services."

She tried her voice. "I'd like to report a robbery at 1233 Morning Beach Drive. It's the condominium complex on the north shore."

"Will you be requiring medical aid?"

"No. No. I just walked in and found my house trashed."

"Then you've had a burglary," the dispatcher comforted, "not a robbery. I'll connect you with the police business office. One minute, please."

The Muzak was so soothing that Teddy realized she was in shock. She looked around. The kitchen was intact. No telling what was missing upstairs. The only real destruction down here seemed to be the tossed salad of books on the floor. The TV was in good shape, Tabor's barbell was in the corner. Just the VCR and sound.

A young woman came on the line, taking her name and address and telling her an officer would arrive soon.

Teddy dashed upstairs and found the bedrooms untouched except for the clock radio. From the upstairs phone she punched in Christian's number.

Busy. She tried again.

"Christian Wells," he said.

"Hi." She was breathless. "I've been burglarized. Could you come down?"

"I'll be right there."

Teddy hung up and trotted down to meet him. He appeared on the patio at nearly the same moment she arrived downstairs.

Sliding open the door, she stepped aside. He looked at the sea of books. "Jesus! How'd they get in?" Answering his own question, he glanced at the torn latch hanging from the doorframe. "These aren't very strong, are they? Did you have your safety bar— Wow!" He picked up the bent aluminum bar and examined the crunch. "This is what the Owner's Association recommends."

"Certainly is."

"Glad I didn't buy one." He set the bar on the table. "What's missing?"

"My V.C.R., stereo components, tapes, C.D.s." She stepped over a pile of books. "I hope they take care of Aretha Franklin."

"Mr. Lloyd's tapes!"

Teddy lifted a book from the T.V. "Gone. But that's okay. I have backups at school."

Christian exhaled. "Did you call the police?"

"Yes."

"Well, that's just about all you can do, isn't it?" He padded back towards the glass door and looked one more time at the lock.

"Wait, Christian. Do you mind staying? I think I'm still a bit rattled."

He wrinkled his brow. "Can't. The answering machine has eight messages and they're all Angela. I'm really in hot water."

"Don't worry, she won't fire you. You're much too valuable."

He gritted his teeth. "Thank you. Let's hope Angela believes that." He held Teddy's eyes and her heart throbbed in her throat. "I'll try to come back later, okay?"

Her front bell rang and he stepped through the doorway, his green eyes already far away. "That's probably the police. I'll let you go."

"Sure. Talk to you later."

"Goodbye."

Teddy opened the door to an Officer Richards from the Bellingham Police and patiently sat with him on the couch while he asked her questions about what was missing, how long she had been gone, and how the door had been locked. When they came to the estimated time of the burglary, she looked at him perplexed. "Is there a way a tell? It could have been any time since yesterday morning."

"More likely last night." Officer Richards looked out at the concrete patio. "There aren't going to be any prints outside." He scanned the room. "Okay, here you go." He picked up her clock radio and plugged it into the wall. "3:32" flashed over and over. "Let's call that 3:30 Sunday morning."

The bell rang again and Teddy stood. "Couldn't be my sister. She doesn't knock."

Padding to the front hall, she looked through the eyehole to see Lieutenant Russell from the sheriff's office examining the city patrol car and the towering aluminum boat in her drive. She opened the door. "Lieutenant Russell."

"You've got visitors."

"Did you know my house was robbed?"

"I just heard. What's missing?"

"V.C.R. and stereo."

"You don't say? May I come in?"

She led him back to the living room and he continued, "Now see what happens when you go away without telling me?"

"I'm sorry. Was I supposed to?"

"I thought that was our agreement."

Back in the living room, Lieutenant Russell of Whatcom County professionally shook hands with Officer Richards from the Bellingham police. Surveying the scene quickly, Russell took in the sliding door and bent safety pole. "Those things might as well be made out of Post-It notes." Looking at Richards, he said, "I didn't mean to interrupt, please go ahead with your report."

"We were just finished." Officer Richards clicked his pen and tucked it in his pocket. "She's all yours." Again the men shook hands and Officer Richards gave Teddy a brochure called "Protecting Your Home." After he had left, Lieutenant Russell smiled merrily and fingered the corner of his sandy mustache, saying nothing.

"We went up to B.C.," said Teddy.

"I know," he said flatly. "I've been waiting for you all weekend."

Teddy sobered. "I'm really sorry we forgot to tell you we were leaving. It came up so suddenly."

"Have a nice time?" He watched her carefully.

"Yes," she said brightly. "We went scuba diving."

"Yes. I guess you did." He looked away to change the conversation. "Actually, what I've been trying to get in touch with you about is your car. I need a look-see. May I?"

"Sure." Leading him out to the garage, she flipped on the light. Parked next to her beige wagon was Tabor's blue Mazda. Without speaking Russell bent down and examined Teddy's tires. "All four of these the same?"

"I don't know. I usually buy two at a time."

He walked around and glanced quickly at all four, grunted, then quickly examined Tabor's.

"What kind are you looking for?" asked Teddy.

He bit his lower lip. "Let me show you." Pivoting on his heel, he pointed to the closed garage door. "Can we go out here?"

She pressed the opener on the wall, and joined him to wait for the door to rumble up the tracks.

Brushing a hand across the soaring silver boat hull as they passed, Russell unlocked the door of the county's white Chevy and pulled out a manila envelope on the front seat. "Come see," he said.

In the envelope were pictures of a white plaster lump imprinted with inky black tire prints. "Know anybody with tires like that?" The prints were an intricate jigsaw of odd tetrahedrons sliced through by four parallel lines.

"Couldn't tell you. I don't usually look at tires."

"They're Toyos. Run 'em on high performance cars."

"They're new, aren't they?" She pointed to the dot-sized protrusions made by the prickly spines from a new tire.

"Very good."

"Are these the ones that went halfway up Margaret's driveway the other night?" There was an engine sound down the street and she looked up to see Steamboat and Tabor pull up in Steamboat's truck.

Russell looked too. "They are indeed."

Tabor leaped from the truck, wild with excitement.

"Lieutenant Russell, we just left you a message. You'll never guess what we found out."

Russell tucked away the photos and gawked at Steamboat. "What's that, dear?"

"We were just returning some air tanks to the scuba shop in the marina and the guy asked where we'd been diving. We said, 'Friendly Cove, it's on the outside of Vancouver Island,' and he said, 'Oh, we just had a woman in here the other day from there.' We knew March had been here because I found this in her boat." Tabor pulled out the hamburger wrapper. "And we said, 'You don't remember which day, do you?' And he said, 'Tuesday. She bought some batteries.' " Tabor emphatically waved the silver wrapper at the deputy. "Do you see? March was down here in Bellingham almost exactly when Margaret was killed. She drove her boat down the coast."

Russell took the wrapper by a corner. "Now, who's this that saw her?" Calmly, he ambled over to examine Steamboat's tires.

"I don't know his name," said Tabor. "Whoever's clerking at Puget Divers right now."

"Tabor," said Teddy. "My house has been broken into. The stereo's missing."

"You're kidding! How'd they get in?"

"Sliding door."

Lieutenant Russell came back and stood beside them. "As I was telling your sister, Tabor, you leave town without telling us and all kinds of bad things happen."

Tabor's face colored. "Oops. We forgot. We just went up to go scuba diving."

Russell closed his eyes to make her prevarication go away. "I know. The Gold River mounties already told us. Wanted to know if any of you had priors down here. Is this the big guy who was with you?" He eyed Steamboat, who extended a hand. "Yes, sir. Jasper Stevens. How do you do."

Russell met the challenge gracefully and withdrew his hand pleasantly surprised. Opening his car door, he leaned on the sill. "Okay, ladies. Let's try again: next time you leave town you come tell me first, okay?"

"Certainly," said Teddy.

"We're sorry we forgot."

They watched Russell drive away and flip on his headlights in the gathering dusk. Teddy brought Tabor and Steamboat inside to survey the damage.

"Feeling violated?" asked Tabor. "That's what everybody says they feel when they get robbed."

"I don't know, it hasn't hit me yet." Teddy turned on a lamp and the bulb popped and died. "AHH!" She shrieked and jumped away. "I don't have any more bulbs!"

"Gee." Tabor put her arm around her sister. "You're really wired. You want me to stay here tonight? I can call Perfecta and tell her I won't make it tomorrow morning."

Stiffly Teddy leaned down and stacked books. "No, I'll be okay."

"I bet we'd all feel better if we eat." Tabor made her way to the kitchen and opened the refrigerator. "When did Aurie say he'd move his boat? I need to get my car out of your garage."

"He didn't."

"Steamboat, want something to eat?" Tabor looked around. "Where's Steamboat?"

"Out here!" he called.

They went out to the garage to find Steamboat sawing the handle off a broom. "We can lay this down in the track of the door." He cut through the wood in four swift stokes. "Maybe it'll do the job for a while."

Teddy stood close as he worked, finding his bulk gently calming. He laid the broom handle in the track and they all retreated to the kitchen where they tag-teamed around the microwave, finishing off leftovers and zapping frozen vegetables. After dinner they loaded Tabor's stuff into the back of the pickup and Tabor nabbed a jar of olives, for the road. Climbing into the passenger seat, she held the jar between her thighs and rolled down the window. "You sure you're going to be okay, Ted?"

"Sure. Christian's coming down in a while."

"Oh, beans. I forgot again: Could you tell Lieutenant Russell I'm moving to Vancouver?"

"Tabor, no."

"Okay, okay. I'll call him when I get there. I really can stay here tonight if you want me to." She looked impatiently through the windshield.

"I'll be fine." Teddy squeezed her sister's shoulder, then watched the red taillights disappear in the dusk.

Back inside, she stood in the twilight surveying the mess in the living room: Tabor's barbell was still in the corner. On the floor by the phone jack the answering machine still blinked. Pressing "Message," she listened to the chirps and waited.

"Hello. This is for Dr. Teodora Morelli. My name is Angela Lloyd Seaver and I'm calling because Christian Wells said you had made some tapes of my father speaking Chinook. I'm trying to prepare his memorial service and I'd like to use some of the old missionary hymns he used to sing when I was a child. I don't know if he sang any of them for you, but if he did, I'd really appreciate being able to get copies, especially 'Amazing Grace.' Some of his old high school friends will be at the service and I know it'd mean a lot to them to hear Chinook again."

Angela paused. "It's noon Sunday and I have to go to the mill. You can call me there at 676-6899, or else later tonight at Dad's." And she gave that number too. "Thank you very much. I hope this won't be too much trouble. And thank you for making the tapes."

The machine burped and cuckooed, then clicked off.

Teddy called Christian's number and found it still busy. Lifting the broom handle with her toe, she slid back the glass door and trotted down the flagstones to his condo.

A fine mist had arrived with the dark, and she raised her cheeks to its silky touch. Clinging to the shadows, she looked in to see Christian clutching his phone, pacing the room like a caged tiger. Round and round his finger he twisted a lock of hair, his vexation plain from fifty feet away. Scuba gear lay abandoned on the floor and creamy file folders were splayed across the dining table. On the wall the grotesque gourmands voyeured like Teddy, mute witnesses of what happens to a busy man who tries to take a weekend off.

Teddy stood stone-still until Christian turned his back, then scurried home to lock the door. Climbing in bed fully clothed, she drew the flannel sheets over her head. That night she dreamed of slaughterhouse chickens, succulent pink muscle washed clean by salty spray.

Next morning in the silver mist, she pulled into the faculty lot to find it entirely empty. Confounded, she turned off the windshield wipers and stared at the speedometer. "Veteran's Day," she said out loud. She thought of her flannel sheets at home, then remembered that she needed the Lloyd tapes for Angela. And some groceries.

She got out and trotted across campus, wintry mizzle swirling like cold hard facts. Passing Media Services she saw that they, too, were closed; another set of backup tapes would have to wait. Upstairs the history department was as quiet as blue mold. Out of habit she checked her empty mailbox, then shuffled books and a portable tape recorder into her satchel. Down the hall in Foreign Languages, she heard laughter in the language lab. She scooped up the Lloyd tapes, locked her door and strode down to see who was there. Peeking in, she nearly dropped her teeth.

"Nigel, hello."

Nigel pulled off his earphones and stood. He was in a padded booth sitting very, very close to Mme. Matejka, the tiny French instructor with slinky cashmere sweaters and long silver cigarettes. Nigel hated cigarettes.

Mme. Matejka stood and smiled. " 'Allo, Ted-ee. 'Ow are you thees morning?'' The woman was positively gloating.

"I'm fine, thank you.'' Teddy clutched her tapes. "You guys are certainly up early for a holiday.''

Nigel opened his mouth but nothing came out. Matejka touched his shoulder possessively and cooed, "Ni-gelle and I were having a disagreement about the accent in Czech at *breakfast* this morning. We're both Czech, you know.''

Balderdash: Matejka's ex-husband was the Czech. And Nigel's old Iowa family was about as Czeched as a damask tablecloth.

Teddy smiled sweetly at Matejka, holding the Lloyd tapes aloft. "Actually, I have a favor to ask. I need copies of these pretty quickly. There aren't any blank tapes around, are there?''

Matejka pushed back her chair. "Of course. Zhere is a whole box in the control room.'' She ducked into the glassed-in booth, her alert little chest leading the way. "If you come here, we can put zem on 'igh speed.'' Her Parisian was charming as hell and she knew it.

Conceding Matejka's victory, Teddy joined her in the control room and watched the artful little woman spin the tapes through the machine. Teddy thanked them both profusely, then shuffled forlornly to the parking lot. She came across a collarless campus mutt frolicking in the rain and explained, "But he was *my* Nigel.''

The dog glared accusingly.

In the rearview mirror she caught her eyes and rehearsed, "I'm just glad you found someone who appreciates you.'' Then: "I'm so glad he found someone who appreciates him.'' Both sentences seemed to resonate properly, but they sure hurt like hell.

Stopping at the grocery store, she came out to find that

the sun had made a surprise appearance. By the time she pulled into Morning Beach, all that was left of the mist was a steaming sheen on the shrubbery. She turned into her cul-de-sac to see Aurie Scholl squatting in her driveway, hitching the rental boat to the back of his Saab. Pulling in, she aimed the garage door opener at him, to jokingly zap him with evil rays. He smiled feebly as the door behind him thundered open.

Parking the wagon, Teddy went out to join him on the drive.

"Happy Veteran's Day," he said.

"You look awful."

Aurie wore a two-day stubble and his skin was ashen: even his earlobes were begging for sleep.

"Guess I do. I just spent the last twenty-four hours peeing in the nurses' hand-held urinals."

"The accident on I-5 was bad?"

"Twelve vehicle pile-up, including a high school drill team from the Kingdome."

"Grim," she agreed. "You should have stayed home and slept if you have the day off."

He nodded toward the garage. "Your sister called and said she wanted to get her car out. And Charlie Tuna wants the boat back." He blinked twice, barely getting his eyes open the second time. "How about you, you guys find March's gold?"

Teddy repositioned her bag of groceries and gestured that he should follow her inside. "Yes, but it wasn't very much, and then March tried to run away with it but the mounties stopped her." Leading him through the garage into the kitchen, she turned on the light. "My house was broken into while we were gone."

"Do you always live like this? Dead women on the linoleum, V.C.R.s out the window."

"How do you know it was my V.C.R.?"

He shrugged. "What else you got?"

They walked into the living room where she had already reshelved most of the books. Those that weren't shelved were piled neatly in stacks ready to go up.

"This doesn't look too bad," he said. "Do you have insurance?"

"I won't make the deductible."

Aurie slumped down on the sofa and took off his glasses. "You wouldn't perchance have an espresso machine, would you?"

Teddy unloaded groceries. "In the garage. I've forgotten how to use it."

"Never mind," he mumbled. "I'll pick up some on the way home." His voice tapered off and when she walked in two minutes later he was asleep. Unfolding an afghan, she laid it over him, which caused his eyes to flutter. "Nice to be here," he said.

There was only one appropriate response, and it seemed to be true: "It's nice to have you." She scooped up her Lloyd tapes and tiptoed into the office.

About 11 a.m. she heard stirring in the kitchen and went out to see. Aurie was banging cabinets, pulling out flour and oil. "Go back to your study, Your Succinctness, I'm making brunch."

"Aurie, you don't have to do that."

"I know, but I'm an incredibly nice guy."

This was Aurie, and he needed rebuttal. "Yes," she said. "I've heard people say that. Oh, wait," she slapped her cheek, "maybe it's only you who says that."

He smiled at the pancake ingredients, happy to be needled. "I was listening to you with those tapes. How long's it going to take?"

"Weeks. Months. I've been dragging my feet because I was afraid I might have the sound of his dying, but I've done three hours so far, and I don't think it's there."

"That'd be nice."

"I know. Right now I'm just popping in and out trying

to find 'Amazing Grace' but I keep getting distracted by his stories. Want to know why '*pelton*' is Chinook for 'fool?' ''

"Ardently, yes."

"Because a clerk named Archibald Pelton who worked for J. J. Astor in Astoria was the sole survivor of a horrible Indian raid. He had a breakdown or something and spent the rest of his life wandering in rags from tribe to tribe. *Pelton*, fool."

"Hear any more about your interviewee?"

"Mr. Lloyd? He's still dead."

Aurie brushed his finger across his chin. "No. I mean about his split lip."

"You didn't like that, did you?"

"Just curious. The Yakima Kid isn't keeping you apprised of all this?"

"The Yakima Kid hasn't had time to put his phone antenna down. I haven't talked to him since yesterday."

"Busy, huh?" He sifted flour into the bowl. "That's too bad."

"You can stop smirking, Aurie. Christian isn't interested in me and he never will be."

Aurie beamed. "What can I say? The boy has no taste." He tapped the sifter. "I wrote you a letter, did you get it?"

She brushed the counter. "You mean the one in which you called your wife a hood ornament?"

Aurie exhaled. "I guess I'm still pretty angry. You're not implying that I could ever think of you as a hood ornament?"

"As I remember, the last thing I got called was 'hysterical,' with all its connotations from second-rate chauvinistic psychology."

"Oh, Teddy." Aurie put down the sifter. "It always comes back to my Isthmus article, doesn't it? Why is that?"

"Because the Isthmus article tells me in a nutshell everything I need to know about Aurie Scholl. When the chips are down, whose interests does he look after: his own, or his own?''

"Teddy, I *did* everything I could. I told my adviser, I told your adviser. I wrote a letter to *Athletic Medicine*.''

"They didn't publish it.''

"What else did you want me to do?''

"Oh, I don't know.'' Her eyes filled with tears. "How about turn around and dump me the next day?''

"Dump *you*?''

She opened her mouth to protest but he kept talking. "Oh, no you don't. You wouldn't even talk to me the whole month of February. You kept leaving the room.''

Her eyes flashed. "Oh, excuse me, I forgot: only surgeons are allowed to get angry.''

"Teddy, what was I supposed to *do*? The way you had it fixed, every time I saw you I was reminded of what a bad person I was.''

"Not you. I was mad at myself.''

He mumbled. "Then Jennifer shows up and I realize at least with her I wouldn't have to worry about appropriating her intellectual property.''

"Appropriating? Is that like stealing?''

"I *won't* use that word. You gave me those articles. You didn't even care 'til after I got published.''

"Not the articles. The ideas!''

"Teddy.'' His voice was quiet. "We arrived at those conclusions together. I remember the conversations distinctly. They were some of the happiest times of my life.''

"I was *feeding* you that! So you would think you were figuring it out yourself.''

"I knew what you were doing and I deliberately put a different spin on mine, so it would be different from yours.''

"Paraphrase,'' she snapped.

He paused. "If you want to think that, that's fine. I'm sorry it appeared that way.''

"And you never even apologized."

"*How many*—?" He shut his mouth, mastering himself. "I can't believe you just said that." In silence he picked up the sifter again, then put it down. "No, this isn't going to work." He turned on the water to wash his hands, getting ready to go.

"What's the matter?" she asked cautiously.

"I just realized that you're going to hit me over the head with '*Verletzungen in Wintersport*' every time we have a conversation, aren't you?"

She bit her lip. "You did apologize, about a thousand times, and I wasn't listening."

"No, you weren't." He snatched the dish towel. "As I remember, you were busy waging war with a tableful of seminar cowboys who couldn't construct a sentence about women in the active voice. Did you *win* your war, Teddy?"

"I can't remember."

"I start feeling mean every time I have to talk about this. Can we just drop it?"

"Sure."

Meticulously he folded the towel and tucked it back on the rack. The silence was thick enough to spread. "I'm not quite sure what happens next."

"I think I try to tell you how much Jennifer hurt my feelings. It blew me away, Aurie. You would *not* believe."

He nodded. "Pain." He regarded her for a full twenty seconds, then said, "I could say I'm sorry again, would that help? I don't know what else to do."

"Thank you. That helped a lot." She turned away.

"Can we be friends?"

"I don't know. Let's talk about it some other time."

"Good." He exhaled and looked at his watch. "So here we are in your kitchen, and it's time for me to go. What do we do now?"

She turned away. "You say goodbye."

"You don't understand. I really, really want to kiss you."

"Do you ever quit, Aurie?" She picked up the mixer like a weapon. "You don't waste *any* time, do you?"

He raised his eyebrows whimsically. "The fact of the matter is, I don't have any time to waste."

"Please go back to Seattle. I can't think about this right now. Besides, we've got a lot to talk about first."

He poked his hands into his pockets. "And I'm so tired of talking."

"You should just go."

"Can't. I came up here to get this straightened out, and I'm not leaving until we get it resolved."

"Get what resolved?"

"Whether you love me or not."

Mortified, she stared. "Damn it, Aurie." Her eyes filled with tears and she put the mixer down. "Don't do this to me."

He waited, his gaze unflinching.

She looked away, collapsing under the pressure. "Aurie, it was so unfair." It came out a sob.

"Oh, Teddy." He crossed the room in two steps, swooping her up onto the kitchen counter. Separating her legs discreetly, he moved between, leaning his weight against the counter edge. Teddy circled his neck with her arms and wept quietly.

"I'm so sorry," he said.

"It's too late, Aurie. I don't think it's anything that can be fixed."

"Sure it can. I'll be smarter this time." He kissed her hair, her forehead, her fingers, and let her cry. Finally she quieted, and he pulled away and said, "I really do have to go. When can I see you again?"

"I don't know." She wiped her eyes. "Why don't you wait a while, then call."

"I can do that. You sure you're going to be okay?"

"Yes."

Through his glasses he looked myopically at her mouth. Without meaning to, she looked at his. Taking off his glasses, he touched his mouth to hers. They kissed, longer than expected, and she remembered his deep, almost female kindness. She thought of his mother and the aunts who raised him, and pulled away to breathe. Realizing they weren't finished yet, she put her face up, waiting to be kissed again. He opened her mouth with his, and the electric shiver of her response was more than she, or he, had bargained for. Wrapping her legs around his waist, she emptied her body to him.

After a moment Aurie pulled away. "Now that was interesting."

"Interesting," she agreed.

His amber eyes danced. "We going to do it again?"

"It wouldn't be again. It would be something different."

Delightedly, they kissed again and he slipped his clever hands under her sweater, running his fingers up the muscles of her back. Desire rushed to her mouth and she remembered the simple pleasure he took in her body.

Again he pulled away. "Everything they say about Italian women is true."

She looked for the golden flecks in his eyes and brushed his hair off his forehead. "Just like everything they say about French Huguenot men."

"I give up. What do they say about French Huguenot men?"

"That—" She began again. "That they're so busy fussing over their own perfectibility, they don't appreciate when other people care about them."

"Horsefeathers. *I* appreciate when other people care about me. What's more, I've got John Donne doing my scout work for me."

"John Donne?"

With ineffable pleasure, he gazed directly in her eyes.

" 'My face in thine eye, thine in mine appear. And true plain hearts do in the faces rest.' "

She grinned.

"Do you want me to go on?"

"I bet you don't know any more."

"I bet you're right." He put on his glasses and glanced over her shoulder at his watch. "I really do have to go."

Teddy hopped down and smoothed her sweater. "I would have to get used to a physician's hours again, wouldn't I?"

He affected a raised eyebrow and suavely grabbed her around the waist. "Don't worry, Ba-bee. I'll make it worth your while."

She smiled weakly.

"What were you thinking right then?"

"Nothing," she said.

"Tell me."

"I was thinking that I would also have to get used to superficial responses to pain."

"Hey, that's not fair." He pulled his bomber jacket off the closet doorknob.

"It might be okay, Aurie. I'd just have to get used to it."

Distractedly they walked down the hall to the front entry. At the front door he zipped his jacket. "You come with demerits too, you know."

"Bull."

"There's those crazy sisters of yours. Not to mention your Holy Roller mother."

"You adore my family and you know it."

"I bet I'm the only person on Infectious rotation who ever had a novena said for him."

"And you didn't catch anything either, did you?"

He tugged at his wrist elastic. "What did Marmee do when Tabor *told* her?"

"Tabor hasn't told anybody yet. She says it's still too soon after Dad."

"What's that been now, three years?"

"Four."

"She's stalling." He opened the door, then bent down and kissed her deeply. "Next weekend?"

Teddy shoved him onto the porch, resenting her own unruly response to his body. "I don't know. Just call."

Outside the day was nearly fair, the drab November sun powdering the shrubbery with silver light. Aurie climbed into his Saab and adjusted the mirrors to accommodate the huge load behind. "Are my brake lights working?"

She watched him wink the red lights of the trailer. "Look fine to me."

"Okay, Stubby, have a good week. I'll call you about the weekend."

"Stubby?" She laughed delightedly. "Aurie, I don't call you names."

"What could be worse than Aurelian? Goodbye, my sweet."

She watched him roll out of the cul-de-sac, maneuvering his gargantuan load. Waiting until he was out of sight, she turned to go back to the house. She glanced down at the drive and jolted to a stop. Bending down, she examined Aurie's tire tracks, and grew numb. Damp against the concrete was an intricate jigsaw of odd tetrahedrons sliced through by four parallel lines.

15

Inside the phone was ringing. She ran back to the living room and dove onto the couch.

"Teddy Morelli," she said.

"Teddy, did Angela get ahold of you?" It was Christian.

"She left a message. She said she'd like to use her father's tapes at the funeral."

"That's what she asked me, too. I'm at work now, but if you want, I can swing by and pick them up."

"Actually, I was going to work on them today. Angela asked for 'Amazing Grace' especially, and it'll probably go faster if I find it myself." She swallowed, waiting.

"Teddy, is something wrong?"

"No, nothing."

"I'm sorry I hurt your feelings yesterday. I'm still really messed up over Jana."

"No, no. It's fine."

He was silent. "Is there something you want to tell me?"

Aurie didn't do it. "No."

"I'll come down later."

She panicked. "No! That's okay. I've got to work on the tapes." She hung up, and the phone rang again. "Damn.

"Teddy Morelli."

182

"Well, hello." It was Lieutenant Russell. "Listen, I was hoping you could help me out."

Aurie didn't do it. "Sure."

"I still don't understand y'all's etiquette. When do I call you Dr. Morelli?"

"Only when I grade your tests, Lieutenant."

He chuckled, folksy and seductive. "Listen, I got two things I want to run by you."

"Fine." Aurie didn't do it.

"First of all, we just had the mounties on the horn and they said that your friend March Hunt was seen at the Gold River airport headed south. We expect she'll clear customs at Vancouver, and if she shows up in your neck of the woods, would you please give us a call? We will also keep a patrol unit out for her."

"Today? Why is she coming to Bellingham?"

"Oh, we don't know she actually is. The mounties just know we're keeping tabs and they called to advise us. Oh, yeah, here you go, this is the other thing I wanted to ask you about: Aurelian Scholl."

She froze. "What about him?"

"He says he's a physician in Seattle."

"That's right."

"Then you know him. What can you tell me about him?"

"N-nothing. He's a good friend. He was with us this weekend up at Friendly Cove."

"What would you say if I told you he called here and suggested we do an autopsy on Walter Lloyd?"

"Aurie? Aurie didn't even know Mr. Lloyd. Did he?"

"Well, I don't know."

"Maybe he was trying to find out if there was incompetence from the nursing staff." Mrs. Dykstra.

"Actually, Dr. Morelli, that's not how we read it ourselves, considering the chain of events."

"What do you mean?"

"I'm afraid when we told the R.N. that a physician had asked for an autopsy she said, good, and be sure to check his blood: she said you may have slipped some medication into Mr. Lloyd's water."

Directly outside her skull, things started to collapse. "But I didn't!"

"Of course you didn't," he soothed, and hung up.

After three attempts she finally cradled the phone receiver. With steely concentration, she walked to the kitchen, made a sandwich, and ate standing up. The turkey stuck to her mouth like peanut butter and she forced it down with a glass of milk. The doorbell rang and she padded to the front hall to find—stupefyingly—her mother standing on the porch.

"Marmee!"

Behind Marmee were her friends Irene Oliveri and Gabriele Zago from church. Irene's red Volvo wagon was parked in the drive. "Hello, Mrs. Oliveri, Mrs. Zago. This is a surprise, come in."

Teddy leaned forward and Marmee graced her with a kiss. Marmee was wearing the blue cloisonne pin at the top of her suit blouse: they'd been doing something liturgical. Her mother's porcelain skin hung softly on her cheeks, refined under its dressing of Lady Esther cold cream and Day Radiance powder. Marmee's eyes were as dark as kitchen espresso, and Teddy held still as Marmee sniffed, taking in all she wanted to know.

"Sodality leadership was in Everett today. Irene said she didn't mind driving up to see you."

Teddy turned to Mrs. Oliveri. "Thanks for bringing her up, I know it's out of the way."

"Nonsense, doll. We heard about you and Tabor. Are you girls all right?"

"I don't know." Teddy looked to her mother, who answered for her. "She's still scared, but she's going to be just fine. Are you sleeping all right?"

"I had nightmares last night."

"Good. That means you're dreaming it through your system." Marmee looked out toward the living room. "You changing your books around?"

Teddy thought for a moment. "Uh-yes. I never had a chance to arrange them properly when I moved in." She hustled them back to the kitchen. "May I make you all some tea? If you don't mind teabags . . ."

Irene tugged off her red driving gloves. "Starbucks has tea bags now."

Marmee slid back a chair and watched Teddy move about the kitchen. Teddy waited. Aurie? The murder? What did she want?

"What's Tabor up to?" asked Marmee.

"Uhh. I'm not sure, Marmee. You know, I *think* she might want to quit grad school, but she's worried that you'll be upset."

"No, Teddy, that won't do. Your brother Carlo taped her Wednesday night on T.V."

"Oh." Teddy mumbled, "Then I guess she's wrestling professionally in Vancouver."

"And this thing with the sailor man, what is she now, crazy?"

Irene interjected kindly, "Tell her it won't work, doll. No matter how hard she tries."

Teddy turned in amazement. "How'd you guys know about him?"

Marmee tossed her head, annoyed at Teddy's dim-wittedness. "You watch the tape: Tabor plants her feet and catches people like that— Sailorman plants his feet and catches people, like that— Tabor raises her fist and shakes it like this, Sailorman raises his fist and shakes it like this." Marmee sniffed. "But that's her barbell in your living room, so I guess she knows better than to move in with him."

Meticulously Teddy set the tea kettle in the middle of

the burner. "Oh, no, that's not Tabor's style at all."

Irene smoothed the wrinkles from the soft red kid. "Teddy, I facilitate for the Women's Integrity group in the diocese, and all I know is that if Tabor thinks she can willfully make herself love this man, all she's going to do is to cause both him and herself a lot of grief."

Teddy arranged tea cups, stalling for time. Finally she looked at her mother. "How long have you known?"

Marmee shrugged. "Since she was four, since she was twelve, since she was eighteen. *Cara*, she's my child."

Gabriele spoke from the corner. "When's she going to tell your mother, Teddy? This has been really hard on Maria."

"Umm." Teddy read the faces as best she could. "She's been afraid of what you'll have to do, Marmee. You'll have to break with either her or the church."

Marmee slapped her purse onto the table. "That's the *stupidest* thing I've ever heard. No one breaks with their children. And the church is stuck. It's been stuck with the Morelli family for the last two thousand years. Now, where does she get these ideas?"

"I don't know."

"Well, tell her to hurry up and tell me. I can't keep this game up much longer."

"Actually." Teddy brightened. "If you want to know the truth, what Tabor would really like is for you to pretend that you've never heard. She kind of likes things the way they are now. She wants you to be proud of her."

"I am proud of her, *cara*. I'm proud of all my children." Tears welled in her eyes.

Irene patted the back of Marmee's hand. "And you've done a wonderful job with them, Maria. Aren't you glad you had your acting to fall back on?"

Marmee sniffed and opened her purse for a handkerchief.

Teddy poured tea and they drank in silence, commenting occasionally on the mallards or the windsurfers, or what

Teddy should buy in the way of small appliances. As Teddy was distributing the last half-cups from the pot, a motion from the patio caught their attention and they looked out to see Christian Wells lifting his hand to knock. Irene tutted, "Will you look at that one." The women watched as Teddy slid back the door.

Teddy set her face so he couldn't tell about Aurie. Brightly, she said, "My mother's here." She led him to the table and made introductions. "Christian, this is my mother, Maria Morelli, and her friends Irene Oliveri and Gabriele Zago. Everyone, this is Christian Wells."

"How do you do?"

Christian gifted each woman with a ravishing smile and politely offered conversation. "Are you just up for the day?"

Irene waved him off. "Go ahead and talk to her, doll. We're finishing here, we'll be gone in a minute."

"That's right." Gabriele gulped her tea.

Christian grinned adorably and turned to Teddy. "I just came down to see if you're finished with the tapes. I was going out to Angela's now."

"Oops, sorry. Still haven't started. I plan to get to them," she glanced at the women, "in a little while."

"We're leaving." Irene opened her purse and twisted up a red cane of lipstick.

Unmoved, Marmee gazed mildly at Christian. "Are you at the college too, Christian?"

"No, ma'am, I work for Lloyd Lumber Company. Your daughter made my employer very happy by recording his Chinook language information just before he died. As far as we can tell, he was the last living Chinook speaker on earth."

"Poor man. When did he pass on?"

"Thursday night."

"Akk! What's happening in this town? Two in a row? And famous people too."

"Coincidence, Marmee." Teddy glanced plainly at the kitchen clock. "Anyway, neither was particularly famous."

"That's not true. Tabor said her writer was the Grand Prize winner of Canada."

"Tabor's batty."

Christian crossed his arms. "She's probably talking about Margaret's Governor General's Award."

"Margaret's?" Marmee used her napkin, then pinned Christian to the wall with her mother's eyelock. "You knew this writer woman too? I thought you were Teddy's friend, not Tabor's."

16

"Christian?" Teddy's heart kicked her diaphragm. "You didn't tell me you knew Margaret Zimmerman."

"Yes, I did. I remember distinctly."

"When?"

"The first night we met. I said, 'How do *you* know Margaret Zimmerman?' Like, I knew her too."

She swept her fingers across the table. "I don't remember."

"Teddy, this is a small town. Margaret applied for a job with us, almost a year ago. I'm sure she applied everywhere."

"You didn't hire her?"

He shook his head. "She wasn't really qualified. She seemed like an interesting lady, though." He looked at his watch. "I really better scoot down the lake. Angela's waiting."

He made his goodbyes and the women watched as he slid the door closed.

Irene did their scouting for them. "What an interesting boy." She let it hang in the air.

"He's just a friend, Marmee."

"I know, *cara*. His heart is somewhere else." Marmee reached for her purse. This Irene took as the sign to slip on her driving gloves. They all stood and Teddy led the way to the foyer. "I hope you don't hit Seattle at rush hour."

"Rush hour is all day, doll. It doesn't make a difference anymore."

Marmee pecked her on the cheek. "We'll see you Thanksgiving?"

"Of course. I'll bring pies."

Her mother winced. "If they don't work out, just buy some. We're having Father Mahoney."

"Rare, or well done?"

"Ha!" Irene squeezed her arm. "Just like your mother."

Outside the women strapped themselves into the red wagon and Irene pulled on a matching red beret. Teddy waved as they drove out of the cul-de-sac, then ran to the phone and called Seattle information. "What number, please?"

"Seattle Orthopedic Clinic."

She called and was immediately switched over to Muzak. After three minutes she had worked out an agreeable descant for Pachelbel.

"Yes?" The receptionist surprised her.

"I'm a friend of Dr. Scholl's and I need to get in touch with him immediately. I believe he's still in his car, if you could possibly give me that number."

Right, lady, next time Mount Rainier sings. "I'm sorry. I'm not authorized to give that information. Would you like to leave a message?"

Very well. She, too, could play hardball. She purred, "Ask him if he would call Teddy back as soon as possible. He knows my number."

"Last name?"

"Ooh, he knows. Do you know how long it will be before he returns my call?"

"We're a little backed up now. We'll get to it as soon as we can." Hey, everybody, Scholl's got a new babe.

"Thank you so much," cooed Teddy. "Tell him it's about his tire tracks."

"Tire tracks?" And guess what, guys, this one's really a bimbo.

"Yes. Thank you," said Teddy.

She exhaled all at once, then dashed upstairs to change into fuzzy sweats. Downstairs again she realized that she would work better in front of the fire. Then, when the fire was lush behind the glass, she discovered she couldn't think clearly unless her living room was back in order. Lugging Tabor's barbell into her office, she waded into the piles of books, reshelving them—this time according to subject.

Standing back an hour later, she saw that the books were no longer handsomely arranged on the shelves, so she racked them again according to color and size, as they had been before. Refueling the fire, she realized she was hungry so she microwaved a potato, ate it, then felt guilty enough to begin work.

Carrying the Lloyd tapes and the college recorder into the living room, she plopped down in front of the fire. Legal pad on her knee, she reset the tape counter to zero and punched on Mr. Lloyd's first singing tape.

The tape hissed. Then there was the sound of rustling papers. "This is Walter MacFarlane Lloyd. It is nine o'clock on Thursday, November sixth. I am at my family home, *Saghalie Illahee*, and I am recording Chinook hymns for Dr . . . Dr. Teodora Morelli of the Rainwater history department. This first song was one used by Methodist missionaries at the reservation, it's called 'Whiskey.' I learned it from Jesse's mother who sang it when she did the ironing."

Teddy noted that "Whiskey" began on cycle 16, then fast-forwarded through the song and punched in and out until she found the beginning of the next song, "Sunday," at cycle 33. Back and forth, she punched the buttons, listening only enough to chart her way through the incomprehensible singing.

At cycle 54 Mr. Lloyd started ''Jesus Loves Me'' and Teddy began situps. When Lloyd finished singing, he turned a page. ''Well, my goodness. Guess what I found?'' His voice warmed with pleasure. ''I just came across the spelling of 'Chinook' as used by Meriwether Lewis of the Lewis and Clark Expedition. Lewis called the language 't-s-c-i-n-u-k,' because they first encountered it in the region of the Chinook Indians along the river.

''Lewis and Clark reminds me of a story told by my grandfather's friend Mr. Klicker of Walla Walla. Klicker used to tell about when he was a boy, how an old Walla Walla Indian who lived on the edge of his father's farm used to tell about when *he* was a boy, how he remembers hiding once in the bushes with his brothers near the confluence of the Snake and the Columbia Rivers watching the first white men they ever saw. They were strangely dressed and very pale, on horses, with *one* Indian woman and her baby—you know who that was, don't you? Sacajawea, with Lewis and Clark. Now I used to believe that story, and maybe I still do—but, you know what? Here's the rub: why didn't he remember Clark's black manservant York? What do you think, gal, you're a historian. Would you remember York if you were an Indian?''

He rattled his pages again. ''Now. These next songs are more secular ones. They were translated—I think—just to tell natives where the white man came from. The first one is 'The Sun Shines Bright on my Old Kentucky *Illahee*,' and then I'll sing 'Good Night, *T'sladie*.' '' Teddy noted the cycle, then wandered out to the kitchen to look for something chocolate.

''Well, what do you know!''

Ice cream carton in hand, she peeked her head back into the living room.

''I can't believe it! I wrote it down! Teddy, get a pencil,

I wrote down what the rain is saying." He paused. "My, that's nice. Okay, ready? I'll leave the translation to you, you've got all those dictionaries. Jesse says the talking rain is saying '*Mika tumtum nanitch*.'" Lloyd repeated, " '*Mika tumtum nanitch.*' Got it? Well, that's nice."

Teddy sprinted across the room and punched rewind, listening to the phrase again. Mouthing syllables, she wrote, "*Mika tumtum nanitch.*"

The Shaw dictionary was in the office so she trotted back to get it. Lloyd had started on "The Sun Shines Bright on my Old Kentucky *Illahee*" but she paid no attention.

> "*Nika illahee, kah-kwa mika*
> *T'see illahee, wake e-li-te,*
> *Kahkwa mika, nika shunta.*"

Abruptly Lloyd stopped singing. "Who's there?"

Teddy looked up from the dictionary.

Lloyd said, "Who let you in?"

There was no answer and he spoke again. "What are you wearing *that* get-up for? Did you windsurf down here?"

Next the tape hissed silence. Then came a cry and the sound of bedsprings. Teddy listened—hair prickly on the back of her neck—to a stifled moan and a crinkly sound, then the kazoolike hum of Mr. Lloyd trying to breathe through a membrane over his face. Jackhammering heart, she stood petrified in the center of the room. Finally she ran over to click off the tape.

"Hello, Teddy." The door slid back and Christian walked in. He was carrying a heavy compound hunting bow with a blue-black arrow nocked onto the string. "Sorry you had to hear that. I've been outside with my fingers crossed, hoping it wouldn't be there."

Teddy's voice wouldn't work. "Y-you killed him."

"And *you* didn't put the broom handle back when you

went for firewood. Fatal mistake.'' He nodded towards the door and a thin nervous man limped in. He had a steel brace on the outside of his jeans and a built-up leather shoe. His hickory-striped logger's shirt was paint splattered but clean, his hair was pulled back into a thick ponytail.

''Teddy, this is my brother Eric, best living artist on the West Coast.''

Eric stuffed his hands in his back jeans pockets. ''Don't say stuff like that, Chris. It's too weird.'' He galumped across the room and ejected the tape from the machine. Holding it up, he queried Christian. ''Wher—'' His voice jumped an octave. ''Where to, Chris?''

Christian's voice was exquisitely kind. ''In the fire. Get the other one, too. It's on the floor.''

Eric grabbed the second tape and laid them both carefully on a burning log. They gave off thick acrid smoke, then, as he prodded with a poker, they curled and melted, disappearing in a bubbly froth.

Christian waited, all the while aiming the wicked arrow at Teddy. On the side of his sleek graphite bow was mounted an open quiver of steely arrow tips catching the light. Teddy tried her voice. ''You didn't have to kill him. He paid you plenty.''

''Let's don't worry about that right now.''

''Foundry bills.'' Eric smiled apologetically. ''Casting in Italy is like melting down money.''

''*Bronzo di Firenze*,'' added Christian.

The best living artist on the West Coast gestured nervously toward Christian's bow. ''What are you going to do? I mean, you can't just let her bleed.''

Teddy gasped, nearly fainting.

Furiously Christian silenced his brother with a glance. ''We'll do the Glad Wrap.'' He waved the ugly bow at Teddy, cooing sweetly, ''Teddy, honey, where do you keep your plastic wrap?''

''Tay-Tay.'' Teddy couldn't talk.

"I'll find it," blurted Eric. Striding manfully into the kitchen, he searched through the drawers and cabinets. Christian called, "If she's got 'heavy duty' that's the best."

Eric banged closed a drawer. "I can't find it, Chris."

Nudging her with his bow tip, Christian pushed Teddy into the kitchen. "Where's your plastic wrap?"

Teddy clutched the counter. The words would not come out.

"*Where?*"

"Tabor won't let me buy it. It's not environmentally c—" She took a breath and blurted, "All I have is waxed paper."

"Shit!" Christian raised his bow to hit her.

"Don't!" Eric grabbed the bow. "Chris, don't. We can't." Tears formed in his eyes.

Christian's face softened. "Eric, look at me. I said look! I need your help on this."

"I can't do this."

"Yes, you can."

Eric wiped his eyes while Christian fleetingly checked his aim on Teddy. "It's going to be okay, Eric. *Mother*'s going to get cast, Gates is going to buy it. You just have to hang in there for this one last one, okay?"

"Can't we just sink her?"

"Oh, right. How we gonna get her down to the water like this?" He meant "conscious" and "well."

Slowly Teddy reached toward the knife drawer. Instantly Christian raised the bow. "You move, I'll shoot. You know I will."

She did know. She brought back her hand.

Drawing back the string, he sighted on her chest, and exhaled professionally. "Eric, go see if she's got duct tape in the garage."

"Yes. Yes." Eric walked in a tight circle, then clumped out to the garage.

Christian, to make his point, took aim through a little

loop imbedded in the string. "With humans I never can decide if you aim above or below the fifth rib. What do you think?"

Teddy stared in terror.

"Tape!" Eric leaped in holding up a roll of silver duct tape. The word sounded like "help."

"Rip off some and put it over her mouth."

Teddy eyed Christian fearfully and closed her mouth to let a jittery Eric tape her lower jaw.

"How about over her nose, Chris? That might, uhm, do it, you know?"

"Can't monitor her breathing like that. This'll be okay, this way she can walk." Christian continued to bead in on Teddy. "And tape her wrists behind, she won't be able to run fast."

"Turn around, please," begged Eric. He grabbed her wrists, and she immediately tensed her forearms, making it appear that her hands would not even come close to touching in back.

"She's not very flexible." Eric tried to pull her wrists together.

"*Umm!*" Teddy simpered through her gag.

"Sorry." He taped her wrists with an eight-inch tether between then, then wound gummy tape over and over around the center strip, until it became a sticky silver shackle. He stepped back to admire his work and Teddy relaxed her forearms. She had at least eight inches of play back there, which was better than none at all.

Eric slid back the glass door and looked into the night. "What if somebody sees us?"

Christian went to the hall closet and took out Teddy's trenchcoat. Slipping it over her shoulders, he taped it across the front. "We're going for a walk. See?"

"I'll go first." Eric slipped outside and Christian pricked Teddy with the black steel point of the arrow. "You stay *right* behind him. If you go anyplace else, you're dead. Got that?''

"Umm."

The rain had turned to night fog. Pale vapor blurred the shadows and strange muted sounds rose from the lake. In single file they walked down to the creaking dock. Eric hopped on, causing the boards to rumble.

"Quiet," whispered Christian. He nudged Teddy. "You too."

They padded to the end where Christian's ski boat thudded softly against the bumpers. Eric untied the lines and Christian pressed Teddy with the arrow tip. "Get in."

Teddy dropped into a stern seat and chill water from the vinyl cushion immediately soaked her clothes. Her nose began to tingle, and panicking, she stood, not knowing how to sneeze with the tape over her mouth. "Hrumph! Hrumph!" Mucus ran down her face.

Christian pushed her back down in the seat. "You just about got yourself killed."

"Wait a minute, she slimed herself." Eric grabbed Teddy's velvet sleeve and wiped her nose.

"Here, take this." Christian handed Eric the hunting bow. "Keep it pulled back and aimed at her left side, got it?"

Awkwardly Eric took the weapon and pulled the cables taut. Closing one eye, he held his hand wobbling by his cheek. "The little loop's to aim through, right?"

Teddy whimpered and held her breath.

Christian started the engine and switched on the bow light to let lakedwellers know that they would be hearing an innocent evening ride. He gunned the throttle and the wind hit so sharply that Teddy's trenchcoat might as well have been hanging in the closet. The tape over her mouth itched unbearably and cramps in her wrists made her want to scream. In high gear Christian streaked comfortably through the fog to the far end of the lake, where the glaciers had scoured the deepest trough.

After intolerable minutes, Christian finally cut the engine and in the foggy silence Eric asked tensely, ''Where's the weight thingie?''

''The anchor, Jerkmeyer. Stay there.'' Christian stepped to a forward hatch and pulled out a mushroom-shaped anchor on a thin nylon line.

Stiffly Eric waved the arrow at Teddy. ''Don't move.''

Christian came stern, squatted in front of Teddy, and ripped the tape off her coat. ''Sit up.''

She sat forward and he stripped the coat from her shoulders. Tying the loose end of the anchor line around her waist, he hanked out fifty feet of nylon rope until it was knotless and untangled, then lifted the lead mushroom at the other end.

''Chris, you should tie her right close to the anchor. If she's far away like that, she'll float up.''

''Eric, please butt out. I've already thought this through.''

''Sure.''

Kindly Christian explained, ''If I tie her close, she's gonna try to hold the anchor and tread water.''

''But this way she—''

''Don't worry. We're in six hundred feet of water.''

White noise rushed in Teddy's ears and her vision blurred.

''Chris, you know what we should have done? We should have brought her purse out too; that way we wouldn't have to go back.''

''Too late now.'' Christian picked up the anchor to plunk it over the side. Suddenly the boat made a sandpaper sound and he lurched backwards. ''Damn it!''

Douglas firs loomed off the bow, their black limbs etched on silver fog.

''Oh, fuck. Reveille Island!''

Eric limped frantically to the bow and squeaked. "I thought you said this was six hundred feet!"

"I overshot. Not a problem." Christian slipped into the driver's seat and started the engine; Eric sat down beside. Neither man looked back at Teddy.

Wild with terror, she stood slightly and slid her bound hands down and sat on the duct tape shackle. Eyeing the men, she stood again and slipped the tape down to the floor, stepping through her bound arms.

"Hey!" Eric lunged.

Fearfully Teddy scooped the neat pile of anchor line over the stern and jammed it into the propeller. Bracing for the moment she would be pulled over herself, she watched the propeller hungrily chew the nylon line, then yank the anchor across the cockpit, pulling it into the water.

The scraping noise sounded like boat-in-a-blender.

"Shit!"

The engine stopped revving and whined like a lovesick cat. Then it only hummed.

"You little bitch!" Christian swatted her with the back of his hand. She fell backwards, landing on the prickly astroturf. Her jaw was certainly broken. He kicked her in the ribs. "God, what a bitch."

"Throw her overboard," Eric barked.

"You bet I'm going to throw her overboard. You just bet." Christian leaned over the stern. "Engine's fouled." He pulled at the tangled line. "It's wrapped around the prop." He leaned farther over the stern, up to his forearms in icy water. "See if you can raise the prop, Eric. It's the switch on the left."

Eric flipped the switch and the engine slowly tilted its whalelike head forward to join them in the boat. Working frantically on the nearly exposed propeller, Christian finally held up a long tangle of line tipped with a ragged nylon end. "We lost the anchor." He glared at Teddy on the astroturf and threw the whole wet tangle of line on her.

Eric inhaled manfully. "Now I see why you have to be such a bastard about this." He picked up the bow and aimed it at Teddy. "You really have to be a bastard, don't you?"

Teddy curled into fetal position.

"We don't have another weight," said Christian. "We're going to have to go back."

"No! Chris."

Christian slid again into the driver's seat. "We don't have any choice. She needs weight to keep her down. And we can get her purse." He tried the key. It wouldn't turn over. "Sh-i-i-t," he said menacingly. He turned again, then again. The engine caught finally and purred.

On the floor, Teddy shivered coatless as they plowed down the lake. They tied up at the dock and Eric came back and nudged her with the arrow. "Walk!" All the way to the house Eric pricked at her back, taunting her with the knife-sharp point.

They slid back the door and Teddy saw that the message light was blinking.

"What's she got that's heavy?" asked Christian.

Eric looked around. "Her V.C.R.'s still in my truck. I can go get that."

"Go look in her garage. We want something small and heavy." Teddy closed her eyes, trying not to think about the barbell in her office. Suddenly Christian shoved her onto the sofa and glared malevolently, not even bothering to aim the bow.

Eric called from the garage, "All I see is an espresso machine. Is that heavy enough?"

"Come back here!" growled Christian. "I'll do it myself."

Eric passed back through the kitchen and stopped in his tracks. "Hey! The microwave. They're heavy."

"Eric, shut up."

"No, I'm serious. Have you ever carried one?"

Christian grabbed Teddy by the arm and dragged her into the kitchen. "Okay, smart ass, how are we going to tie a line to it?"

"Timber hitches. Didn't you ever see my show with the body bags?"

Christian went back to get the bow. "Teddy," he barked. "Pick up the microwave."

Still gagged, hands now tethered in front, Teddy slid the microwave to the front of the counter and lifted it off. "Umm." The weight was so unwieldy she pushed it back, waiting for their wrath.

"Eric, you're going to have to carry it."

"No, she can do it." Eric pivoted the microwave on the counter. "Weight's in the back. You just need it next to your body."

Teddy picked up the microwave again, finding the heaviness now bearable.

Suddenly out in the entry, the front door rattled as someone tried to let himself in.

"Sh-h." Christian handed Eric the bow and tiptoed over to close the kitchen door to the hall.

The doorbell rang, then someone knocked.

"Quick," whispered Christian. He led them to the sliding glass and pushed it open. "Not a word," he snarled to Teddy. "Eric, get behind her with the bow."

Struggling under the weight of the microwave, she followed Christian down the flagstones, her arms quivering uncontrollably. The chill made her teeth chatter and her feet were so cold they felt like stubs. Behind her Eric pricked the arrow point relentlessly into her back. Halfway to the dock, Teddy tripped and fumbled, dropping the microwave. Falling to her knees, she pleaded to Christian with her eyes.

Christian leaned down and picked up the faux walnut box. "What a wimp."

They proceeded to the dock, when suddenly, from around the boathouse, came a voice. "Hey, Teddy." It was

Tabor. "What are you guys doing?" She walked over slowly, eyeing Eric, who casually lowered the bow. Joining their little circle, Tabor found nothing to say. They waited in thunderous silence.

"That your microwave?" Tabor asked.

No one answered.

"I'll take that, Bozo." Steamboat—from out of nowhere—thwacked Eric across the forearms, and the hunting bow tumbled to the ground. Dropping the microwave, Christian made a lunge for the bow. Steamboat calmly planted his foot on the bow cables and bludgeoned Christian backward with a sweep of his bearlike paw. Christian landed on his rear and Steamboat looked back and forth between the brothers.

Grabbing Eric by the ponytail, Steamboat dragged him over to Christian and snatched Christian's ankle as he tried to scoot backwards in a crabwalk. Deftly twisting the ankle a half turn, Steamboat waited for the physics to apply themselves as Christian turned over on his belly. Eric thrashed and slapped, batting awkwardly at Steamboat. "Don't," barked Steamboat, and he jerked the ponytail to show Eric why he shouldn't.

"Tabor?" he called. "Can you take the skinny guy?"

Tabor was instantly at his side. "Sure, Steamboat, what do I do?"

"Just a minute. Let me fix Christian first." Still dragging Eric by the hair, Steamboat arched Christian's leg up behind his back, pressing Christian's chin into the grass, and his body into a graceful backwards curve.

"Aaurgh!" bleated Christian.

"Yeah, man. It's very important you not move right now, we could rupture a lumbar vertebra. You going to hold still for me?"

"Aaurgh!"

Teddy watched as Christian grasped for the bow near Steamboat's feet. "Hmm!" she called through the tape. She looped the bow cables around her foot and dragged it off.

"Thank you, Teddy." Steamboat turned to Tabor. "Okay, now, let me teach you my Boston crab." Holding Eric at arm's length, he offered him to Tabor. "But first we got to bring him down."

"How do we do that, Steamboat?"

"Okay. First you take his wrist and twist—no, other way—while pressing your thumb between the metacarpals. Right there, yeah, get 'em good and flattened out."

"Ow!" howled Eric.

"Sorry, man, she's new at this."

Eric obediently bent over forward, his braced leg stretched out to the side.

"Steamboat, what about his leg brace?"

"It's better than normal. It'll go all at once. Okay, now, get his thumb flexed out, let him know who's boss. Quiet you!" he barked at Christian. "Good, Tabor, now you got him. Okay, keep twisting, torque him on over to his back."

With minimal prompting, Eric planted his head on the ground, did a somersault, and lay gratefully on the grass.

Tabor looked up triumphantly. "Now what?"

Lights went on in the condos and people came onto the patios. "Is everything okay down there?"

"No," shouted Steamboat. "Call the cops!"

Face on fire from the adhesive, Teddy bent over and grasped the bow, then scurried toward the lighted houses.

Lieutenant Russell leaned against Steamboat's truck and watched forlornly as a city patrol car pulled out with Christian and Eric in the back. Turning to Teddy, he examined her face. "You're going to have a burn there, gal. You sure you don't want to go to the hospital?"

Teddy touched her cheek with cold fingers and pulled the aluminum med-evac blanket closer. "I'll use ice." She stretched her jaw and found that, although sore, it still worked perfectly at the joint.

The neighbors began wandering away, and Steamboat came out carrying Tabor's barbell. "I hate to think about what would have happened if we hadn't come back for this, Teddy."

Teddy watched as Tabor unhitched the tailgate and Steamboat set the bar in his truck bed. "Me, too."

Tabor latched the gate. "I don't understand why they killed your old guy in the first place. Wasn't he about to die anyway?"

A taxi entered the cul-de-sac.

Teddy answered, "Christian was stealing from Mr. Lloyd to finance Eric. I guess he thought Mr. Lloyd was about to find out." She stomped back and forth. "Can we go in? My feet are freezing."

They mounted the porch and the taxi pulled up directly in front of her condo. From the back seat, a wiry, silver-haired woman leaned over to berate the driver.

"Holy cow," said Tabor.

March Hunt climbed from the taxi, clumping over in her Vibram-soled boots. "Freddy, I found you. Girlie," she greeted.

"Lady?" called the driver.

March scrutinized Russell in his blue gabardine. "Officer, pay my fare."

"A—"

March waved her hands irritably. "I came all the way down here and all I'm asking for is taxi fare. Go on, I don't keep money."

Stunned, Russell took out his wallet and paid the driver. Walking back warily, he eyed March.

"Now," March began. "Does anybody know what windows are?"

"Windows?"

Deep from the pocket of her fog-colored sweater, March pulled out two floppy disks. "My sister called me Saturday, last week, ranting like a loon. I hadn't talked to her in years and when she asked me to come down to see her, I was flabbergasted. I thought maybe she had changed her mind about the treasure—incidently, Girlie, I found this in the pocket of the valise.''

She pulled out a slim spiral pad and dangled it in front of Tabor. ''Margaret *was* writing a treasure story, or had at least taken notes on one. And here, Freddy, here's your Chinook list, you forgot it.''

Teddy unfolded the paper.

saltchuck—saltwater
skookumchuck—rough water, white water
potlatch—potlatch

She turned it over, looking for more.

''Where was I?'' said March. ''Oh, yes. Margaret. After she called me last weekend I boated down the outside coast, got here Tuesday, and met her at the harbor where she refused to talk about the dolls, said she was in profound danger and pressed these disks on me.

''She said she had been working as a secretary for a place called''—she read from the disk—''Lloyd Lumber Company. The manager was stealing and he fired her when he caught her snooping in the accounts.

''I asked why she didn't go to the police and she said she hadn't built a case yet, but that these,'' March handed the disks to Russell, ''were a start. I hope you know what to do with them, because I certainly don't. Margaret said to give them to someone in authority, and tell them they needed 'Windows.' ''

March climbed the front steps. ''Freddy, I'm going in your house to use your flush toilet. You may make me tea if you like. I take it with milk.''

17

St. Paul's Episcopal was a study in contrasts. Swelling in the front pews was a sea of Burberrys, and Teddy looked on, wondering if she wasn't viewing the whole 39 percent bracket of Bellingham.

In the center of church were Lloyd mill workers—outdoor men standing close to their wives, so as not to miss subtle behavioral cues. And finally, across the back were Lummi elders. They wore plaid woolens and plain eyeglasses, and were more attuned to the sense of ceremony than the brocaded priest himself.

Craning her neck around Tabor's body, Teddy peeked to the front pew to see the stunning woman in black Armani with a fat Chanel bow in her hair.

The organ sounded and they all rose. Teddy had never found "Amazing Grace," and now they opened the hymnals and sang it for themselves. Afterwards they listened to the readings, as the New Testament tried to justify itself to the Old.

Next the priest himself climbed the winding steps to the pulpit. From his eulogy they learned that Mr. Lloyd had rowed crew at the University of Washington after World War II, and was the youngest climber of Mount Rainier at age thirteen. At twenty-four he had won the heart of the beautiful tennis-playing Stonie Bradburn of the Seattle

Bradburns, but only after conceding that she would always be able to beat him at the game. In later life Lloyd had quietly funded AA chapters and county libraries, sometimes even carrying entire charities by himself.

It was a rich life they heard; it made them laugh and cry. When the priest was finished, he bowed his head and waited, and a tape hissed gently over the sound system. Then, in a breathy baritone, Mr. Lloyd sang once more.

> *"Ahnkuttie nika tikegh whiskey*
> *Ahnkuttie nika tikegh whiskey*
> *Pe alta nika mash*
> *Alta nika mash.*
> *Alta nika mash."*

Heads bobbed and smiled, many wiping away tears. In the pew next to Tabor, Steamboat took a fountain pen from his pocket and scribbled notes on the back of his memorial pamphlet.

Afterwards they stood straddling the kneelers, watching people approach Angela, offering their condolences and basking in her exquisite presence.

"You want to go introduce yourself?" asked Tabor.

"I don't think so. She looks awfully busy."

Steamboat leaned over. "Of course you'll go. We'll take you." He guided her out of the pew. "You know, Teddy, I wouldn't mind listening to those songs you taped. Could I do that?"

"Sure. They're public property."

"I have a friend on Vancouver Island with a recording studio. They still use a few Chinook words up there. Might be a market for those songs."

They waited in line, mesmerized by Angela's elegant response as she greeted old friends. When it was their turn, Steamboat acted as spokesman. "Mrs. Seaver, this is Dr. Teddy Morelli of the Western history department and her sister Tabor. Teddy did the recordings of your father—''

''Dr. Morelli, of course.'' Angela extended a willowy hand. ''And you also found Mother's china. Thank you so much.''

''You got it back?''

''Oh, yes. The tea set, too. An old classmate of Dad's works at Home Care Nursing and she persuaded Mrs. Dykstra that it might be in everyone's best interest if it found its way back home. I don't think anyone's feelings were hurt.''

Tabor asked, ''Have they been able do anything with Margaret's floppy disks yet?''

Clouds gathered in Angela's beautiful brown eyes. ''The sheriff's department had me in there twice yesterday. Every file we open up is more appalling than the last.''

Tabor finally asked for them. ''Like what?''

''Like, one of them called 'Payroll' is a list of all the personnel and their Social Security numbers. But there were men on that list that I remember dying *years* ago. We're still tracking, but the sheriff told me that Christian probably had them set up as dummy employees and pocketed their checks himself. Then another file called 'EPA' shows that thirty-six thousand dollars that should have gone to toxic waste disposal was put into something called 'Central Cleanup Fund,' whatever that is.''

''Not Jesse's company, I assume,'' said Teddy.

''Jesse? Who told you about him?''

''Christian, without meaning to. I guess he set Jesse up independently so he could steal from him. Is that right?''

''We think so.'' Angela's eyes watered. ''Jerry Montague from the mill said he thinks Christian had ordered Jesse to dump our penta in the woods rather than truck it down to the toxic waste site in Arlington, Oregon.''

''And siphon off the disposal money himself?'' asked Steamboat.

"We assume, yes. We're in terrible trouble with the EPA."

Teddy said, "I should probably talk to Lieutenant Russell. I might know a little about that from a conversation I overheard."

Angela nodded. "Would you? They've decided to open a homicide investigation into Jesse's death now. Most of Jesse's friends say it was highly unlikely that he passed out in the kiln. They said he'd been dry for years."

"Then that would make three murders, wouldn't it? Jesse, Margaret, and your father."

Angela pulled a lacy handkerchief from her sleeve. "It's overwhelming, isn't it? But as Lieutenant Russell pointed out, the only evidence they have of even one crime is what's on your tape."

"You mean there are no fingerprints, or anything, at your Dad's?" asked Tabor.

Angela patted the corner of her eyes with the handkerchief. "We'll see." Her eyes were not hopeful. "Christian's been awfully clever. Yesterday they found that the laser security light across Dad's balcony door had been taken down and put back six inches off the floor."

"Maybe they'll find something out at Margaret's farm now that they know what they're looking for: the weapon, maybe."

"Hey!" said Tabor. "His diving knife."

Angela shook her head. "They don't think so. Down at the sheriff's office I saw a whole baggie of marquetry tools tagged as evidence. X-acto knife blades and some handles. But Lieutenant Russell says he probably threw away the one he used."

"Do they know what Margaret did that alarmed him?" asked Tabor.

"No. Probably the same thing that gets everybody— I.R.S. We found a tax file in the office full of paperwork for Margaret. She was the one who had to deal with the pension deductions and Social Security numbers, and evidently she had alerted the tax people without realizing how serious the consequences would be for her. I just hired a new accountant and she says we're going to have to file for an extension to sort it out.''

A hovering man in a black suit touched Angela lightly on the elbow. Smiling cordially, she readjusted the kid bag on her shoulder. ''I think we have to go. Thank you so much for everything.''

''We're awfully sorry about your dad.''

''Yes, thank you. Thank you for everything.'' Angela disappeared into a sea of dark woolens.

18

Aurie poked an alder log in the fire, then rolled over on his back to look around the book-lined room. Out in the violet air, rain plummeted like a trout stream, flooding the downspouts and forcing mallards up the lawn.

"Why don't we call Seattle and tell them I've moved my practice up here to your dining room table?"

"Good idea." Dropping the xeroxed Chinook dictionary, Teddy stretched on the rug like a cat. "Tabor can run the rehab unit in the living room and I'll sell espresso in the kitchen. Full service, Northwest."

"What a nice offer." He reached for her hand and put it to his mouth. "I've always known you cared."

"Aurie, you're so full of it." She pulled her hand away.

"I know." He sighed. "Very important in a surgeon."

Looking into the fire, she asked, "What did you tell Lieutenant Russell on the phone?"

Aurie shrugged. "Same thing I told you: that I was out there looking for Tabor, and I only went halfway up the drive because it was killing my suspension."

"I knew you didn't kill Margaret."

"And you just said that out loud, what does that mean?" He reached for the Chinook dictionary and thumbed the pages. "You know what else Russell said?"

"What?"

"All the jail personnel are taking turns to work Christian's wing. They're very impressed."

"Why?"

"He says typically a killer uses the same method over and over again, and that's how they catch him. But Christian changed M.O.s each time. So, basically they're handling a guy smarter than they are, which they don't see very often in jail."

"M.O.s," She tested the word, then watched the blue base of a flame. "I have another question."

"Shoot."

"When you asked Russell for Mr. Lloyd's autopsy, did you already know Christian had killed Mr. Lloyd?"

Resting the dictionary on his chest, Aurie took off his glasses and rubbed his eyes. "I'd love to claim prescient knowledge if it would impress you, but actually I was just trying to bail you out."

"Me?"

"Yeah." He rubbed his chin with his finger. "I'd never heard of a stroke victim biting his lip before, and I figured if he really died from a seizure, somebody screwed up his medication and was trying to blame you by saying you caused a stroke."

"Thank you for requesting an autopsy. That was very thoughtful."

"It's my nature."

Rolling on her side, she propped herself up on her elbow. "I should have been suspicious of Christian when he wanted to go away with me for the weekend. I knew he wasn't interested in me."

"The flawed judgment of the young."

She shook her head. "My vanity aside, what he really wanted was to get me up to Vancouver Island so Eric could take the Chinook tapes out of here. Christian must have been just dying over those tapes. He was there the other morning when Mrs. Dykstra said they might have recorded the sounds of Mr. Lloyd's dying. Can you imagine?''

"Poor guy. Serves him right. Speaking of Vancouver Island," said Aurie, "did Steamboat ever find out what happened with Bailley and the gold?''

"He says the B.C. government will probably keep it. Bailley and the Nuu-chal-nulth have filed land claims for most of the island, but at this point the cove is still crown land." She sat up cross-legged and stared into the fire.

"Maybe we can go see Jewitt's gold at the Provincial Museum someday. Unless March figures out how to poach it back.''

"She's sad, isn't she?''

"What do you mean?" he said. "I think she's incredible.''

"In what way?''

"Well," said Aurie, "she's arranged her whole adult life so that it successfully copes with a horrific childhood. And far as I can tell she hasn't self-destructed, or hurt anybody else in the process. Done it on sheer willpower.''

Teddy looked into the fire. "I keep thinking about her, about when she and Margaret were little girls." She turned to watch the thin dictionary on his chest rise and fall with his breathing. "What I don't understand, though, is why little-sister Margaret didn't grow up to be as tormented as big-sister March. I mean, they had the same mother, the same experiences, but as far as I can tell, all Margaret did was use it for material: you know, lemonade from lemons.''

Aurie shrugged. "Just shows you can't predict the outcome of the same events on different people. Or maybe it shows the difference between 'big sister, little sister.' I don't know, too many variables.''

"I wonder if because Margaret was the baby, she got all the love and attention . . .''

"Or maybe their mother was more amenable to child-rearing by that time, did a better job.''

Teddy plucked the dictionary off his chest. "We need to

get back to work on this talking rain. '*Mika tumtum nanitch*.' '' She opened the book and was immediately lost in the antique print. ''Now that's interesting. Did you know 'salt' didn't exist as a concept until whites brought it in?''

Aurie snatched the dictionary. ''This is going to take all night if you do it.'' He turned to the ''M's.'' ''Okay, *mika*. *Mika* means 'you' or 'your.' ''

Grabbing a pencil, Teddy scribbled on a pad. ''So I could say, '*Mika* Aurie?' ''

''You could say anything you want. But the last man on earth who knew if you were correct just died.''

''Go to the next word. '*Tumtum*.' That's a weird one.''

Aurie turned to the ''T's.'' '' '*Tumtum*,' wow, loaded word: 'will, spirit, heart, intellect, soul.' There's an etymology note here. '*Tumtum*: Onomatopoeic, from the pulsations of the heart.' Gee, I haven't thought about onomatopoeia in years.''

''Lots of Chinook words are onomatopoeic,'' said Teddy. '' '*Wawa*,' 'to talk.' '*Lip-lip*,' 'to boil.' ''

''*Mika tumtum* what?''

''*Nanitch*.'' He flipped pages. '' 'Perceive or listen.' ''

Teddy read from her pad. '' 'You will listen; Your spirit, listen.' Big deal, you could say anything.''

''You're being too literal. A good translator has to turn it into poetry.''

''Oh, the poetry doctor. Excuse me.'' She handed him the pad and pencil.

Drawing an editorial ''S'' curve through her sentences, he said, ''It's a dictum, so obviously the verb comes first.''

''Perceive your soul, listen to your will,'' she tested.

''Better.''

''Listen to your soul.''

The fire popped and Aurie said, ''Look up '*tumtum*' again.''

Flat on her back, she read to the ceiling: '' '*Tumtum*: will, spirit, heart, intellect, soul.' ''

He scribbled for a moment on the pad. "Okay, I've got it. Lucretius would be proud."

"What?"

"How about this: The talking rain is saying '*Mika tumtum nanitch*,' which translates, 'Listen to your heart.' "

"Aurie, I like it."

"I like it, too."

He dropped the pencil and they gazed at the fire. Outside they heard the drumming in the downspouts and the sheeting of the wind.

ACKNOWLEDGMENTS

John Jewitt's fascinating narrative of massacre and captivity among the Nootka has been in print continuously since his return to Boston in 1807. Currently, the most accessible telling of his story is Hilary Stewart's annotated edition, *The Adventures and Suffering of John R. Jewitt, Captive of Maquinna* (Douglas and McIntyre, Vancouver/Toronto, 1987).

For assistance with the Chinook and Captain Cook manuscripts I am extremely grateful to Special Collections, Allen Library, University of Washington; the Bellingham Public Library; and Librarian Virginia Beck of Special Collections, Western Washington University.

Special thanks also to Canadian historian Dr. Cecelia Danysk; the Mow-ach-achts Band of the Nuu-chal-nulth; Mike Paris and Rod Palm of the Underwater Archeological Society of British Columbia; the Vancouver Maritime Museum; local historian Polly Hansen; wrestler Nick Kiniski; scuba diver Tom Shaffer; Allen Scott of Yeager's Archery Department; the Gold River Library; Jason Sheasby; the Bellingham Police Department; Ian Thompson M.D.; reader Anna Mariz; agent Jane Chelius; editor Andrea Sinert; and copy editor Lisa Eicher.

Born in New Orleans and raised in Atlanta, LINDA FRENCH lives in a college town in Washington state. She is trained in American history and has worked as a community college instructor, grants administrator, and creative writing teacher. A former Georgia state backstroke record-holder, Linda's favorite recent purchase is a black rubber wetsuit for swimming in Puget Sound. She is currently at work on the next Professor Teodora Morelli mystery.

Explore Uncharted Terrains of Mystery
with *Anna Pigeon, Parks Ranger* by

NEVADA BARR

TRACK OF THE CAT
72164-3/$6.50 US/$8.50 Can

National parks ranger Anna Pigeon must hunt down the killer of a fellow ranger in the Southwestern wilderness—and it looks as if the trail might lead her to a two-legged beast.

A SUPERIOR DEATH
72362-X/$6.50 US/$8.50 Can

Anna must leave the serene backcountry to investigate a fresh corpse found on a submerged shipwreck at the bottom of Lake Superior—how did it get there, and, more important, who put it there?

ILL WIND
72363-8/$6.99 US/$8.99 Can

An overwhelming number of medical emergencies and two unexplained deaths transform Colorado's Mesa Verde National Park into a murderous puzzle Anna must quickly solve.